# FREDDY *the* MAGICIAN

## The Complete FREDDY THE PIG Series
### Available or Coming Soon from The Overlook Press

# FREDDY

## *the*

# MAGICIAN

*by* WALTER R. BROOKS

*Illustrated by Kurt Wiese*

THE OVERLOOK PRESS
NEW YORK, NY

If you enjoyed this book, very likely you will be interested not only in the other Freddy books published in this series, but also in joining the *Friends of Freddy,* an organization of Freddy devotees.

We will be pleased to hear from any reader about our "Freddy" publishing program. You can easily contact us by logging on to either THE OVERLOOK PRESS website or the Freddy website.

The website addresses are as follows:

THE OVERLOOK PRESS
www.overlookpress.com

FREDDY
www.friendsoffreddy.org

We look forward to hearing from you soon.

This edition first published in paperback in the United States in 2011 by

The Overlook Press, Peter Mayer Publishers, Inc.
141 Wooster Street
New York, NY 10012
www.overlookpress.com
For bulk and special sales, please contact sales@overlookny.com

Dust jacket and endpaper artwork courtesy of the Lee Secrest collection and archive.

Cataloging-in-Publication Data is available from the Library of Congress

Brooks, Walter R., 1886-1958
Freddy the magician / Walter R. Brooks ; illustrated by Kurt Wiese.
p.  cm.

Manufactured in the United States of America

ISBN 978-1-59020-481-8

2  4  6  8  10  9  7  5  3  1

# FREDDY *the* MAGICIAN

*. . . it did look sort of awful.*

## Chapter 1

Pigs are not generally thought of as very tidy animals, and I suppose a good many people would have been surprised to see what Mr. Bean's pig, Freddy, was doing the morning after the big gale.

The tail end of a hurricane had whipped across the Bean farm, tearing limbs off trees, ripping shingles off roofs, and strewing everything that wasn't nailed down over half a mile of countryside. The whole barnyard was littered with twigs and even good-sized branches, and the little terrace in front of the pig pen, where Freddy sat and dozed on drowsy summer afternoons, was a mess. So Freddy was cleaning up.

He picked up all the rubbish and carted it off in the little rubber-tired wheelbarrow that Mr. Bean had given him last Christmas and then after resting a while he went down to the house to borrow a broom. All the other animals were at work tidying up the barnyard, and on the roof of the house Mr. Bean was nailing on new shingles in place of those that the wind had torn off. Mrs. Wiggins, one of the cows, had hooked a horn into a big branch that had blown off the crabapple tree and was dragging it away. She stopped when she saw Freddy.

"I don't suppose you've had any word from Centerboro yet, have you, Freddy?" she asked.

Freddy shook his head. "No. I thought after we got through here, maybe some of us could go down to the circus grounds and give Mr. Boomschmidt a hand. The place must be a shambles after the storm."

"I've never seen a shambles," said Mrs. Wiggins, who had no idea what the word meant, "but probably you're right. I must say I'm glad we went to the circus Tuesday. I'd hate to have been in that big tent yesterday when the storm struck."

The circus was paying its yearly visit to Centerboro. The Bean animals always went to it in a body, for the proprietor, Mr. Boomschmidt, was an old friend and always gave them free seats. Indeed, Freddy had several times gone on the road with the show and taken part in the performance, and he had many close friends in the menagerie. I suppose that Leo, the circus lion, was as close to him as any of his own relatives. So the Bean animals were naturally worried about what might have happened when that high wind struck.

"I was planning to go again tomorrow," said Freddy. "That new magician that's with the show—he's wonderful! I'd like to get him to give me some lessons. Of course I could never do card tricks; you have to have hands for that and I've got trotters. But I bet I could learn some of the others. Maybe I could give performances."

"Well, I hope you won't," said the cow. "I should be nervous as a witch when you were around if I thought any minute you might take an egg out of my ear, or fire off a pistol and make a canary appear in a bird cage. And sawing that girl in two—that was downright wicked, Freddy."

"Oh, he didn't really saw her in two," said Freddy. "There was some trick to it. Anyway, you saw the girl afterwards, didn't you? So he couldn't have hurt her."

"How do I know it was the same girl?" said Mrs. Wiggins. "It looked like her, but it might have been her twin sister."

"He saws a girl in two at every performance," said Freddy. "So there'd have to be about a hundred girls all looking just alike—a hundred twin sisters. Only you wouldn't call them twins if there were a hundred of them, would you?"

"Hundreduplets, I suppose," said the cow. "Just the same I don't see how there could be any trick about it—he certainly sawed her in two. I just don't think it's right. And anyway . . ." She stopped.

"Look, there's Mrs. Bean calling to us."

The two animals crossed the barnyard to the back porch, where Mrs. Bean was standing. Mrs. Bean was small and plump and comfortable looking and she had red cheeks and snapping black eyes, and the animals were all very fond of her. They were fond of Mr. Bean too, but he was harder to get acquainted with because he didn't talk much and because you never could tell what he was thinking on account of the whiskers that covered up his expression.

Mrs. Bean said: "Freddy, now that everything's about cleaned up after the storm, why don't you and some of the others go down to Centerboro and help Mr. Boomschmidt? He phoned a while ago and said if we could spare any of you, he'd be very grateful. He said there was nobody hurt; everybody got out of the big tent all right; but some of the smaller tents were blown to pieces and a lot of stuff scattered around."

"Mrs. Wiggins and I were just talking about going down," Freddy said. "If it's all right with you and Mr. Bean, I'll collect some of the others and start now."

Down at the Centerboro fairgrounds everybody was hard at work straightening up after the storm. Men and animals were rushing around, mending torn canvas and tightening guy ropes and picking up and sorting out stuff that had been scattered by the wind. On the top of a very tall stepladder in the middle of everything sat Mr. Boomschmidt, his plug hat on the back of his head, shouting orders through a megaphone at the various gangs. Every now and then when he shouted too vigorously, his hat would fall off, and when that happened, Jonesy, the giraffe, who was standing beside the ladder, would pick it up and hand it back to him.

When Mr. Boomschmidt saw the Bean animals come through the gate he waved and then shouted greetings at them through the megaphone. He swept off his hat and bowed so low to Mrs. Wiggins that he overbalanced and would have bounced right down the steps of the ladder if Jonesy hadn't propped him up again. Then supporting himself with a hand on the giraffe's head, he said, "Welcome, animals! Welcome! My goodness, you're certainly real friends. But I'll thank you later. Just pitch in wherever you're needed, will you? And Freddy, do go over to Leo's wagon and see if you can't cheer him up. Gracious, you haven't heard about him? Why, you know how proud he is of his mane. Well, the wind started the wagon he lives in rolling down the hill, and instead of jumping, he stuck with it and it ran off the road and overturned in a big patch of weeds and threw him out. He wasn't hurt any, but oh, dear me, is that mane of his a mess of burrs! He sat up all night trying to comb them

*"Quit being so sorry for yourself, Leo."*

so, Freddy? More masculine, eh? Well, perhaps there's something in it. Only . . . only . . . suppose I don't? Suppose I don't like it?"

"OK, suppose you don't," said Freddy. "Then you get a false mane made. A wig."

Leo let out a roar. "Me? Wear a wig? Are you crazy?"

"Now take it easy," said Freddy. "Lots of great people—kings and movie actors and so on —have worn wigs."

"Yeah?" said Leo. "Name one."

"Well, Louis Fourteen was the King of France and he wore a wig. And so did Louis Fifteen and Sixteen."

"And Seventeen," said Mrs. Wiggins, trying to be helpful.

"Never even heard of Louis One," said Leo. "Try again."

"Well, how about George Washington?" said the pig. "He wore one."

"He wore knee pants, too," said Leo, "but that's no reason why I should."

"Oh, all right, all right," said Freddy crossly. "Have it your way. That's the thanks we get. Come on, Mrs. Wiggins." He turned away and ran smack into a tall thin man in a dress suit who had come up to the lion cage.

The pig drew back and bowed and said politely: "I beg your pardon, sir. I'm afraid I didn't see you."

The man had sharp black eyes, very white teeth under a black moustache that curled in two little horns up on either side of his nose. He wore no hat but around his shoulders was a long black cape, lined with red. "Not at all," he said. "Not at all. Most people, I find, are singularly unobservant. They go through life not seeing many things that are right under their noses. Permit me." And he reached out a hand and took a silver dollar out of Freddy's left ear. "Not under your nose exactly," he said, "but in the immediate vicinity. Been there for weeks, I dare say, and you've never noticed it.— And you, madam," he said, turning to Mrs. Wiggins, "I'm sorry to see that you haven't combed your hair recently." He picked an old bird's nest and a small bouquet of paper flowers from between her horns. "Tut, tut! Very slovenly. You ought to be more particular about your appearance."

"Oh!" said Freddy delightedly. "You're Signor Zingo!"

"In person," said the magician with a self-satisfied smile.

Freddy said: "I saw your performance Tuesday and it was—well it was wonderful!"

"Naturally," Signor Zingo said. "Naturally. A performance that has been given before all the crowned heads of Europe, that has won deafening applause in every first-class theatre from London to Bombay, from Capetown to Reykjavik, that has charmed the distinguished drawing rooms of three continents . . ."

"Modest little man, isn't he?" Leo interrupted sarcastically. "That's what I like about you, Zing—so many people brag about their accomplishments, but not you! No sir, just a shrinking violet."

The magician showed his teeth in a tight smile. "Ah, yes, Leo," he said; "we're rather alike in that, aren't we? You've been rather shrinking from the public gaze too since yesterday, haven't you? Very wise of you, I must say, with that donkey's breakfast you call a mane on your head. King of the Beasts, hey? You look like the King of the Scarecrows." He narrowed his eyes viciously at the lion, and Freddy, who had at first thought he might be rather nice, didn't like him any more.

Neither did Mrs. Wiggins. And like all cows, she never hesitated to speak her mind. "Look here, Mr. Zingo," she said. "Maybe Leo hadn't ought to have said what he did about your bragging, but it isn't very nice of you to make fun of his mane when he's so upset about it. If you want my opinion, I think you're just plain mean!"

Signor Zingo turned on her. "Oh, do you, madam! Well, since we're exchanging opinions, may I say that your fat silly face gives me acute indigestion? And please take it away."

Cows are plain and there is nothing they can do about it, but they are very kindhearted animals, and it is a pretty mean man who will deliberately insult a cow. Mrs. Wiggins was hurt and astonished. "Well I never!" she exclaimed.

Freddy was good and mad. Mrs. Wiggins was not only his partner and one of his oldest friends, she was a lady, and Freddy had been too well brought up not to resent an insult to a lady, even if a perfect stranger. He showed his teeth in a snarl that would have done credit to Leo. "See here, mister," he said; "you take that back and apologize. Quick!"

"Ha, chivalrous pig!" said Signor Zingo contemptuously. "And what will you do if I don't? Tear me limb from limb?"

People who don't know much about pigs are

not likely to class them as dangerous animals; but an angry pig is something that no farmer in his senses will tackle barehanded. One snap of Freddy's strong jaws could have taken a good-sized chunk out of the magician. And Freddy was just about to rush when he was interrupted by Mr. Boomschmidt, who had climbed down from his ladder and come bustling over.

"Come, come, Zing," he said. "I heard that last remark of yours. A very ungentlemanly remark, very ungentlemanly indeed. This lady is a friend of mine, an old friend. If you have to insult somebody, why can't you insult somebody I don't like? Why don't you . . ." He laughed suddenly—"Why don't you insult yourself, hey? I don't like you very well, you know." He doubled up with laughter, and Freddy and then Mrs. Wiggins, and finally Leo, began to laugh too.

Signor Zingo didn't laugh. He kept the tight little smile on his face, and really looked quite dangerous. "Very witty, Boomschmidt," he said. "Being my employer gives you the right to say what you please, of course."

"Dear me," said Mr. Boomschmidt, "I always say what I please, Zing. Though what I say doesn't always please me after I've said it. Well now, and that's funny too, isn't it? How do you explain that, Leo? Eh?—Or no, never mind; you're not feeling well this morning; forget that I asked you. Now what is this all about?"

They all began talking at once, but after a moment Mr. Boomschmidt put his fingers in his ears. "Oh dear," he said, "you're just mixing me up. I think the best plan is for you all to apologize all around and start fresh. Eh? You first, Zing."

"I won't be the first," said the magician.

"Well, I certainly won't," Leo said.

"Mrs. Wiggins and I have nothing to apologize for," said Freddy.

"Just the same, as a favor to me, you'll apologize if the others do, won't you?" Mr. Boomschmidt asked, and when they nodded he said: "Now I'll count three and when I say 'three' you'll all say: 'I apologize.' Agreed?" So he counted and then when they had all mumbled together: "I apologize," he said: "Come along, Zing; I want to talk to you about that hat."

"I will gladly come with you," said the magician, "if you'll persuade this—this lion to return to me the comb I lent him last night to get the burrs out of his mane."

"But I keep telling you, Zing," said Leo: "I lost the comb. I can't find it."

"You haven't been out of your cage all morning. It must be there somewhere."

"Of course it's here," said Leo. "It's in my mane somewhere. But if you can find it, you're a whole lot smarter than I think you are. And I don't think . . ."

"Now, Leo!" said Mr. Boomschmidt warningly.

"All right, chief," said the lion. "I'll tell him what I think later. But he's been pestering me for that comb—and it only had about four teeth anyway. But I'm perfectly willing to buy him another."

"Well, if it's in his mane," said Mr. Boomschmidt, "my gracious, Zing, go on in his cage and help him find it."

Leo laughed. "Yeah, Zing, come on in. Come into my little parlor, and come out in pieces, in fragments, in little tiny chawed-up bits." He spread the claws of one big forepaw and raked it across the floor of the cage so that the splinters flew.

Leo was one of the mildest lions in the world, and Freddy knew that he wouldn't hurt Signor Zingo no matter what the magician said. But Signor Zingo hadn't been with the circus very long and didn't know that Leo's cage had no lock and that the lion could have come out any time and chewed him to mincemeat if he had wanted to. So he backed away from the cage and said with a contemptuous look: "Let him have the comb if he wants it." And he walked away with Mr. Boomschmidt.

"Well!" said Mrs. Wiggins. "What an unpleasant man!"

"Yes," said Freddy. "And there go my magic lessons, darn it!"

Arm in arm, Mr. Boomschmidt and Signor Zingo were walking towards the big tent. Suddenly, at something Mr. Boomschmidt said, the magician jerked his arm loose, stopped, and turned to stare back at Freddy. He asked a question, and when Mr. Boomschmidt had answered, he started to walk slowly back towards the pig, while Mr. Boomschmidt went on into the tent.

Freddy stood his ground. The man didn't look as if he intended to start any trouble; he looked puzzled and thoughtful. But when he had come about half the distance back, he stopped again, shrugged, and turned off in another direction.

"That's funny," said Mrs. Wiggins. "I thought he was going to say something to you."

"It was something Mr. Boomschmidt said that started him back here," said Freddy. "I'm going to find out." And he started towards the big tent.

Leo opened the door of his cage and came out. He picked up the blanket that Freddy had pulled down and wrapped it around his head like a shawl. "I'm coming along with you," he said. "I guess you're right, Freddy; it's the clippers for me. The chief's got a pair and I'll get him to run 'em over me."

"My goodness gracious me," said Mr. Boom-schmidt when they caught up with him. "How can I remember what I said to him? I never pay any attention to what I say to people."

"I should think you could remember that," said Freddy. "It was only a minute ago."

Mr. Boomschmidt pushed his hat back on his head and thought. "No," he said. "No, it doesn't come to me. You see, Freddy, it is the things that people say to me that are important —not what I say to them. Those are the things I remember."

"All right," said the pig. "Then what did Zingo say to you, just before he stopped and turned around?"

Mr. Boomschmidt answered promptly. "He

said: 'So he's that detective I've heard so much about, is he? Well, well; I wish I'd known!' "

"I see," said Freddy. "Then you must have told him that I was a detective."

"I suppose I did," Mr. Boomschmidt said, "but as I told you, I don't ever listen to what I say myself. I don't suppose I even hear it. That's perfectly natural, isn't it? Don't you think it is, Leo? After all, what I want is to hear what the other fellow says."

"Sure, chief, sure," said the lion. "But now look—do you want to run those clippers over me? I guess it's the best thing. I can't go on like this." He shook his head sadly. "But I don't know where I'll ever get the courage to face my looking glass."

## Chapter 2

When they left Mr. Boomschmidt, Freddy and
Mrs. Wiggins joined one of the gangs that were
cleaning up the circus grounds. After they had
worked a while, the cooks who prepared the
meals for the circus people came out carrying
big freezers and a lot of plates and spoons, and
everybody knocked off and had ice cream.

This was an idea of Mr. Boomschmidt's, and
it was one of the reasons why people liked to
work for him—he was always giving them little
surprises.

Freddy licked his plate clean and lay back in the grass. "I wonder why that magician started to come back when he found out we were detectives?" he said.

"Maybe he's committed some crime," said the cow. "Maybe he thinks we're after him."

They puzzled over Signor Zingo's strange behavior for a while, but could find no explanation for it, and were just thinking about going back to work again when a rabbit came hopping up to them. He wasn't anybody Freddy knew. All the rabbits on the Bean farm were sort of light tan color, but this one was pure white. He said: "Good morning, sir. Are you Frederick of Frederick and Wiggins, the famous detectives?"

"I am," said the pig, "and this is my associate, Mrs. Wiggins." He looked sharply at the rabbit. "I've seen you before somewhere. Wait a minute," he said. "I know who you are. You're the rabbit that Signor Zingo took out of a silk hat during his performance Tuesday."

"I see, sir," said the rabbit, "that you are indeed as clever as people say you are. A brilliant piece of deduction, if I may say so, sir."

Freddy liked praise as well as most people but he thought the rabbit was laying it on pretty thick. "Nonsense," he said gruffly; "there's nothing very brilliant about recognizing some-one you've seen before. I looked carefully at that hat trick. And by the way, how does he do it? Do you really disappear?"

"Oh yes, sir. Absolutely invisible. I'd gladly show you how it's done if we only had the hat. But it blew away. It's lost. And that is why I came over here—to see if you wouldn't help me find it."

"I wouldn't help that boss of yours find his hat if he offered me a thousand dollars. I wouldn't help him find it if he crawled up to me on his knees and knocked his forehead on the ground three times and rubbed ashes in his hair. I wouldn't . . ."

"You mean you won't help me?" said the rab-bit. "Oh, dear!" And his ears, which had stuck up straight in the regular rabbit position, began to droop. They began at the tips and went slowly down, like little window shades, until they hung straight down beside his head, mak-ing him look terribly forlorn.

"My land," said Mrs. Wiggins, "that's quite a trick!"

"It's not a trick!" said the rabbit sharply. "My ears always do that when I'm unhappy."

*"It is not a trick!" said the rabbit sharply.*

"That's interesting," Freddy said. "Now when I'm unhappy, the curl always comes out of my tail. But of course," he said kindly, "you haven't much in the way of a tail."

"I have too," the rabbit retorted, "and it isn't all twisted up like a pretzel, either! But forgive me," he said, "I didn't want to start an argument. I—well, I was sure you'd take my case; first, because it's an extremely difficult one, and second, because it's extremely unusual. And everyone tells me that as a solver of really difficult cases, there is no one to equal you. I am sure that with your brilliant deductive powers and your wide knowledge of animal nature . . ."

"Skip the flattery," said Freddy. "We do like difficult cases, but we don't like Signor Zingo, or his hat, or his rabbit, or anything that belongs to him. And so—"

"But I don't like Zingo either," the rabbit interrupted. "He fired me. He said I was no good to him without the hat. And when I asked him how I was going to live, he just laughed and said: 'Go fend for yourself. Rabbits can always live off the country.'"

"Well, can't they?" Mrs. Wiggins asked.

"I suppose so, if they're brought up to it. But I'm a magician's rabbit. I don't know how."

"That was pretty mean—kicking you out after you'd worked for him a long time," said the cow.

"Can't he get another hat?" Freddy asked.

"He said such hats were too expensive—he couldn't afford it. And that's the reason I came to you: he said if I could find the hat he'd take me on again."

Freddy shook his head. "I'm sorry," he said, "but we don't take out-of-town cases any more —just do local detective work for our friends, and that keeps us busy. Besides, I intend to take up magic and conjuring this summer, and I won't have any extra time."

"Magic!" said the rabbit. "Well, if you want magic, there's nobody who can teach you more about it than I can. Can't we make a deal: you take my case and I'll teach you magic?"

"Could you show us how Signor Zingo saws that girl in two?" Mrs. Wiggins asked eagerly.

"Sure. Nothing to it. I can teach you all those tricks."

Freddy said: "H'm," and the rabbit's ears went halfway up. "But on the other hand . . ." said Freddy, and the ears went down again.

"Let's hear his case anyway, Freddy," said the cow.

Freddy said: "I'm not specially interested in sawing anybody in two. I wouldn't care to try it on anybody I liked, and on anybody I didn't like it would be sort of a waste of time, since apparently they don't stay sawed. But we can hear your story."

The rabbit's name was Presto. He was called that because when Signor Zingo made him appear out of a hat, he always said: "Presto, change-o!" He came of a long line of disappearing rabbits: his grandfather had worked for Houdini, and both he and his father had worked for Zingo.

This hat trick was one of the most difficult in all magic, Presto said, because it was real magic, not like making a girl disappear from a cabinet, which was done by having her climb down through a concealed trap door in the floor. "When I get into the hat and then disappear," Presto said, "I *really* disappear, you understand."

"Good land," said Mrs. Wiggins, but Freddy said: "Yeah. Sure. Well, go on."

Well, it seemed that when the hurricane struck the circus, Signor Zingo was just packing up his magic apparatus. The trick silk hat was on the table beside him. And the wind came in under the tent and scooped up the hat, along with some papers that were on the table too, and took it out of the door, and the last that was seen of it, it was flying through the air above the treetops in a northwesterly direction, and the papers were flying around it like a lot of white pigeons following a big black crow.

"Well, the hat ought to be easy to find," Freddy said. "Now, wait a minute," he said as Presto's ears went quickly all the way up; "I'm not saying we'll take your case: I'm only suggesting how to go about finding the hat yourself."

"I could never find it," said Presto. "Oh dear, if you'd only . . . I'll teach you everything— all the tricks there are. Please, sir!"

And so after some more argument, Freddy agreed.

Mrs. Wiggins was pretty impatient with Freddy for hesitating so long, and when they had sent the rabbit away, with a promise to pick him up when they left and take him back to the farm with them, she said: "I don't see why you told him we had so much to do; we haven't had any detective work in two months. Didn't you really want his case?"

"I intended to take it all the time," Freddy

said. "Only, if I'd let him see that we wanted it, he wouldn't have thought we were very good detectives."

"My goodness," said the cow, "we're in the detective business, aren't we? We advertise for cases in the Bean Home News, don't we? It seems sort of silly when someone comes to offer us a job to pretend we don't want it."

"Well, that's the way you have to do business," said Freddy. "If somebody comes to buy something you have to sell, you don't just give it to him right away. You pretend you don't know whether you want to sell it to him or not. And the more you put him off, the more determined he is to buy. It's like being in love."

Mrs. Wiggins said: "I've never been in love."

"Well, neither have I," said Freddy. "But the principle's the same."

"What principle?" said Mrs. Wiggins, looking puzzled. Then she said: "Oh, never mind. I just think it's a very funny way of doing business. It doesn't make sense."

"It may not make sense, but it makes sales," said the pig.

## Chapter 3

When the detective firm of Frederick and Wiggins got back to the Bean farm they were met just outside the gate by the black cat, Jinx.

"Hi, sleuths!" he called. "Got any good clues today? Say, you're a hot pair of detectives all right. How about getting your homework done before you go gallivanting off to the circus grounds?"

"What do you mean, homework?" Freddy asked, and Jinx said: "I mean there's detective work for you right here on the farm, and you two walked off and paid no attention to it. Come along." He led them through the gate and then stopped. "Now stand right still here a minute; take a gander at the old layout. See anything wrong?"

The animals were still busy around the barn-yard, but most of the litter had been cleared away. Mr. Bean had come down from the roof and was tightening the screws in the hinges of the stable door.

"I don't see anything," said Mrs. Wiggins, and Freddy agreed. "Looks a little neater than usual, that's all," he said.

Jinx grinned. "Boy, oh boy! What a pair of dopes! Look around. Don't you miss anything?"

They shook their heads, and Mrs. Wiggins said: "Good land, don't be so mysterious, cat. If you've lost something and want us to find it, why not say so?"

Suddenly—"The henhouse!" Freddy exclaimed. "Where on earth is the henhouse?" They all looked across the barnyard at a bare strip of earth where yesterday the small but handsome building with its little revolving doors had stood. "And Charles! And Henrietta!" Freddy went on in a shocked voice. "And all those darned little chickens! That's right;

I didn't notice them around this morning; but you mean to say—?"

"Yeah," said the cat; "I mean to say that we were all so blamed busy this morning cleaning up after the storm that not one of us noticed that the henhouse was gone. And it wasn't until Mrs. Bean came out to look for eggs that we discovered it. Blown away in the hurricane, and probably floating around in the middle of Lake Ontario by this time, with Charles standing on the roof and making one of his speeches to the wild waves. And the perch and the pickerel playing merry-go-round with the revolving doors."

"Good grief!" Mrs. Wiggins exclaimed. "This is no time to be funny about it! We must find out where they are."

"They probably wouldn't come to much harm," said Jinx. "They've got wings; if they get blown into the air they can always get down easy."

"Well, come on," said Freddy. "What are we waiting for? We only have to follow the wind. It came from the southeast, so we'll send a search party out to the northwest. Hey, Mr. Pomeroy!" he called to a robin who was listening for worms at the corner of the garden.

The robin hopped over. He wore spectacles which made him look like a small owl.

"Look, J. J.," said Freddy. "Will you get in touch with all the other birds and ask 'em to scout up northwest and see if they can locate our henhouse? It blew away in the hurricane, and we're worried about Charles and his family. It can't have gone very far, and I don't think it will be hard to find. And—oh, yes; ask them to keep an eye out for a hat, a black stovepipe hat like the one Mr. Boomschmidt wears. That's missing, too. It may be a lot farther away than the henhouse, but Mrs. Wiggins and I are offering a generous reward to the one that finds it. Just broadcast that, J. J., and report to me in the cow barn if there's any news."

When the robin had flown off, Freddy went in to see Presto, who had been entertaining Mrs. Wiggins' sisters, Mrs. Wurzburger and Mrs. Wogus, with a few simple tricks. The cows were delighted with the charming manners of their guest, and had told them that they hoped he would make his home with them for as long as he liked. Freddy was not surprised at this. He had seen that Presto was a great flatterer, and neither Mrs. Wurzburger nor Mrs. Wogus ever got much flattery. Very few people ever bother to flatter a cow. "I'm afraid it won't be very exciting for him," Mrs. Wogus said to Freddy, "for we live very quietly, but if he cares to stay we will be only too happy to have him."

"Their kindness quite overwhelms me," Presto said. "There is so little that a poor lonely rabbit has to offer such highly cultivated ladies. I hardly know what to say."

"I guess you'll find something to say all right," said Freddy drily. "Well, if they want to put you up here, it's all right with me. But in the meantime, suppose we start in on those magic lessons. Come on over to the pig pen."

So they went over into Freddy's study, and Presto began by explaining some of the easier tricks that he had watched Signor Zingo do. Freddy saw very quickly that there wasn't any use trying to do tricks with cards or any other sleight-of-hand feats. These depended on nimble fingers, and for a pig, who has no fingers, they were impossible. But there were a lot of other tricks that were worked by means of secret pockets, and by clips and other pieces of apparatus fastened inside the magician's clothing, and Presto assured him that he could learn to do these very easily. So Freddy selected, from the row of hooks on which were hung the various disguises he used in his detective work, an old suit of Mr. Bean's which Mrs. Bean had cut down for him; and with some pieces of cloth and with needle and thread he went to work under Presto's direction to make himself a magician's coat.

They had sewn in several secret pockets, and had made a number of clips out of wire and fastened them in under the lapels and inside the sleeves, when there was a light tap on the window and they looked up to see Mr. Pomeroy standing on the sill. Freddy let him in.

"Well," said the robin, "we've located your henhouse. It got blown all the way up to Otesaraga Lake, and it landed in a big pine tree on your friend Mr. Camphor's estate. My Cousin Isabel lives up there, you know, and she saw it and talked with Charles and Henrietta, and flew down to tell us about it."

"Good gracious," said Freddy, "how terrible!"

"Oh, I wouldn't say that. I guess it was quite an experience, for the house turned over several times while it was in the air, but it landed right side up and nobody was hurt. Henrietta sent word not to worry—that they were all well and really enjoying a nice vacation."

From his window Freddy could see that Mr. Bean had hitched Hank, the old white horse, to the buggy and was evidently just about to start off on a search for the henhouse. Although he knew that his animals could talk, Mr. Bean never liked to hear them. He said it was unnatural and made him nervous. There are a lot of people like that. Anything a little out of the ordinary disturbs and frightens them. But this was an important matter, so Freddy ran out and told the farmer what he had learned. "And I think, sir," he said, "that it might be a good idea if Mrs. Wiggins and I went up there and brought you back a report on just how things are. Then you can arrange for getting the henhouse out of the tree and back here."

Mr. Bean stared hard at the pig, puffing on his pipe; then he gave a grunt—which was his way of agreeing with anybody—and began unhitching Hank from the buggy. And Freddy ran to get Mrs. Wiggins.

It was a long trip up through the Big Woods and across country to the lake, and it was suppertime before they reached Mr. Camphor's house. Mr. Camphor was in Washington, but he had left word with his butler, Bannister, that whenever Freddy and any of the Bean animals came they were to be treated as honored guests. So Bannister said they must certainly have dinner and stay the night, and what would they like to eat?

"Good land," said Mrs. Wiggins, "don't fuss for *me*. All I ever have is a little grass and a bucket of water."

So Mrs. Wiggins had her dinner outside, but Freddy went in and ate a hearty meal.

Afterwards they walked down to the lake shore and Bannister showed them the henhouse. There it was, perched in the upper branches of a huge pine overhanging the water, and looking as if it had always been there. They could hear chicks chirping, and the scolding voice of a hen, but when Mrs. Wiggins rapped on the tree trunk with her left horn, there was sudden quiet, and then Charles, the rooster, came to the henhouse door and looked down.

Charles was delighted to see them and he called Henrietta, and they both hopped down from branch to branch until they reached the ground. "Natural staircase," said Charles. "Rather neat, eh? I do wish you could come up and see our view. Really, you know, we were extremely fortunate to find such a charming location."

"You sound as if you'd picked it our your-selves," said Freddy. "But how about coming home? The Beans are pretty worried about you."

"Home?" said Charles. "But this *is* home—this henhouse. Penthouse, I should say. You don't suggest that we should move back to that noisy barnyard? All that traffic and racket! Here it's quiet and peaceful and the breeze every evening just rocks the house gently so the children go off to sleep without any fuss. When the wind blows the penthouse will rock, you know."

"Yeah," said Freddy. "And when the bough breaks, the henhouse will fall."

"Dear me," said Henrietta, "after our expe-rience in the hurricane we don't worry much about that. I'm sorry about the Beans, though. But if you tell him that we're all right and that we're going to stay, I'm sure he'll understand."

Mrs. Wiggins and Freddy looked at each other. "Well," said the pig, "it's up to you. We'll tell him how things are." They knew there was no use arguing, so they let Charles show them around. He spoke with such pride and elo-quence of the beauties of the estate, that a stranger listening might have thought he had just bought the place from Mr. Camphor. And his plans for the future rather carried out that idea. He was going to do this, he was going to do that; he was going to have a little boat on the lake and teach the children to swim . . .

Presently it began to grow dark, and Henrietta said they must be getting home; they wouldn't be able to see their staircase after dark. So the two animals said good night to them and went back to the house.

"Mr. Bean isn't going to like this," Mrs. Wiggins said.

"You bet he isn't," said Freddy. "But I don't know what we can do. You see how determined they are to stay here. And you know how pigheaded Charles can be. Goodness—pigheaded!" he exclaimed. "There I go using that word again! Pigheaded! I'd like to get hold of that Noah Webster for about five minutes—I'll tell him a few things! He's the one that caused all the trouble: putting words like that in his dictionary! I bet I could sue for libel or something."

"Well," said the cow, "we only have to wait for the first good rip-snorting thunderstorm. You know how scared Charles is of lightning.

*"Home?" said Charles. "But this is home . . ."*

They'll come hotfooting it home as soon as they can get there."

"That's all right," Freddy said, "but the Beans will worry about them. They ought to come home now. I wonder . . . I think maybe we can work it. Let's go in and have a talk with Bannister."

So they had a talk with Bannister, and then they talked together for a while, and then Bannister showed them up to the guest rooms he had prepared for them. Freddy had the Blue Room, and Mrs. Wiggins had the Ancestors' Room, where the portraits of all Mr. Camphor's ancestors were hung.

At daylight next morning Charles came out of the henhouse door. He hopped up to the highest twig of the pine tree, and as soon as the top edge of the sun glittered above the horizon, he crowed. At the third crow, Bannister's head popped out of an upper window. "Stop that racket!" he shouted.

"Don't be silly," said Charles. "The sun's coming up. I always crow when the sun comes up."

"Not on this estate, you don't," said Bannister. "Mr. Camphor doesn't allow any crowing on his property."

"Nonsense!" said Charles superciliously. "I'm afraid you're not very well informed. It is the unalterable custom of all roosters to salute the dawn with appropriate musical notes."

"Yeah?" said Bannister. "Well, it's *my* custom to salute it with this musical note." And he reached inside and brought out a shotgun, and aimed it well over Charles' head and pulled the trigger.

The gun made a terrible bang; and the dozens of shot zipped and whizzed around Charles' head. The rooster gave a squawk and almost fell out of the tree; then he scrambled down from his twig and into the henhouse door. "Henrietta!" he shouted. "I'm shot! Get a doctor right away! I'm dying!"

Now of course all this had been arranged the night before, and Freddy and Mrs. Wiggins hurried down to the pine tree. Henrietta, finding that Charles was, of course, not wounded at all, boxed his ears soundly, then went outside and began telling Bannister what she thought of him. He was a murderer and a dangerous criminal and she was going to call the police and wait till Mr. Camphor got home and heard about this brutal attack on his guests. . . . But Bannister had shut the window, so finally Henrietta stopped.

"This is terrible, Henrietta," said Mrs. Wiggins. "Just when you were getting settled in your nice new home. What are you going to do?"

"I don't know," said the hen, "but we're certainly not going to stay here!"

Freddy shook his head gloomily. "It's too bad. Well, I'll go back and talk to Mr. Bean; maybe he'll let you come back. But I wouldn't count on it."

"Take us *back!*" Henrietta screamed. "What are you talking about, you silly pig? Of course he'd take us back if we wanted to come." And Charles, who had finally decided that he wasn't going to die heroically of his wounds, came out beside her. "Not take *me* back—the most talented singer in the state? He'd jump at the chance."

"Well," said Freddy, "it's rather embarrassing, but . . . I suppose I ought to tell you. When the Beans found that you were gone, they —well, they didn't seem very much upset. Indeed, they . . . Oh, I'd better just tell you what they said. It was that they felt it would be a lot quieter and more peaceful around the barnyard with you gone. 'All that everlasting cackle,' Mrs. Bean said, and Mr. Bean—you know how he does—just nodded and puffed his pipe and said: 'M-hm, m-hm. Untidy critters.' "

"Untidy!" exclaimed Henrietta. "Me? That's the best housekeeper in—"

"I'm only telling you what they *said*," Freddy protested.

"And why didn't we hear anything of this last night?" Charles asked.

"We saw no reason to tell you then," said the cow. "You were going to live here, and . . ."

"Charles!" said Henrietta. "Pack up your things. We're going back there at once. I'm going to have this out with the Beans once for all. Untidy indeed! I'll get the children ready."

## Chapter 4

The next day Mr. Bean went up and got the henhouse. It was quite a job. He got some of the neighbors to help him, and they rigged a block and tackle and swung the house out of the tree and down to the ground, and then loaded it on a truck and brought it home.

That evening Charles gave a lecture in the barn on *My Experiences in the Big Blow.* You wouldn't think he could make much of a lecture out of it, for all that had happened was that he had heard the wind blow harder and harder, and then the henhouse had gone up in the air and turned over three times and come to rest. And when Charles got over being dizzy he staggered to the door and looked out and there was a lake. But he made a story out of it that lasted two hours. Indeed he would have talked all night if at the end of the second hour he hadn't noticed that his audience had gone home. He had talked the barn empty although it had been full when he started. Except for Hank, who was drowsing in his stall, only Jinx was left, curled up in a corner asleep. The cat woke up when Charles' voice finally stopped.

"Ho, hum!" he yawned. "All through, Charlie, old fowl? Well, want to hear now about *my* experiences in the Big Blow?"

"*Your* experiences!" said Charles contemptuously. "Nothing happened to you! You were safe in the house under the stove all the time."

"I'm not referring to the late hurricane," said the cat. "I'm speaking of your lecture. Ha, talk about wind! Compared to you that hurricane was nothing but a mouse sneeze!"

"Very funny," said Charles, and stalked with great dignity out of the door.

Freddy and Presto had attended the lecture, but had left even earlier than the others to go back to the pig pen and continue the magic lessons. Freddy was practicing making small objects disappear. He had a piece of elastic, one end of which was sewed fast up inside the sleeve of his magician's coat. On the other end was a little clip which he could fasten to a coin or a pencil or anything of the same size. Then, with Presto as audience, he would pick up a coin, and while he was handling it and talking about it, manage to fix the clip to it. Then he would hold it out as if about to give it to the rabbit. Presto would make a snatch for it, and Freddy would let go at the right moment and of course it would disappear right up his sleeve. On about the twentieth repetition the trick was beginning to go quite smoothly, when there was a knock at the door. Freddy opened it and admitted Leo.

"Whoo!" said the lion. "Stuffy in here. What you got everything shut up on a fine summer night like this for?"

Freddy didn't answer. He held out the coin to the lion. "Take a look at this," he said.

Leo reached for the coin which at once disappeared. "Well, dye my hair!" he exclaimed. "That's a trick and a half! But it isn't a good one for the president of the First Animal Bank to be doing. People won't want to let you take care of their money for them if you make it disappear as quickly as that." He glanced sharply at Presto. "How about making that rabbit disappear, hey? I've a private matter I'd like to discuss with you."

"Oh, sir," said Presto, "I was just going. Good night, Mr. Freddy. And may I say, sir," he said, pausing at the door to address the lion, "how very becoming your new haircut is? Very distinguished. Quite regal in fact."

"You may say anything you want to," said Leo, "as long as you say it on the other side of the door." And he grabbed the rabbit and unceremoniously shoved him outside.

"Aren't you being a little hard on him?" Freddy protested. "My gracious, Leo, you do look nice with your mane clipped!" he said as the lion came forward into the circle of lamplight. "It's a great improvement. Don't you think so yourself?"

"Well, yes and no," Leo said. "It's cooler and of course it's a lot less trouble and expense. But I keep having a feeling it isn't *me*. You know what I mean? When I pass a mirror or a store window—you know how you just glance in to see if you've got any egg on your chin, or if you're looking as dignified as you think you are? Well,

I catch sight of myself and for a second it sort of scares me."

"You mean you think it's another lion?"

"Not exactly. It's sort of hard to say just what I mean. You see, when I see myself, I think I look one way, and then I find out that I look quite different. And it makes me wonder if when I think I look sort of noble I'm not really looking just sort of half-witted. Like when I'm talking to you, now, for instance—I think I look probably worried, but reasonably intelligent. But—do I? I just can't be sure. Maybe I'm really making idiotic faces at you. You got a mirror handy?" And he looked around anxiously.

"You look all right," said the pig. "And it isn't a good idea to be watching yourself in mirrors all the time. Oh, I know, I know; I do it myself a lot. Everybody does. Except possibly Mr. Bean, who can't see himself anyway behind those whiskers. I know how it is, sometimes, when you're talking to people and you begin to worry that maybe your face has got out of control and your features are sort of wandering all over and making you look as if you were doing monkey imitations. But mirrors don't help much."

*"How very becoming your new haircut is."*

"They help me," Leo said.

"Not really," said Freddy. "You, being a lion, I suppose want to look dignified and interesting, with just a little touch of ferocity. I, being a pig, want to look clever and good-humored, with just a dash of romance. Probably neither of us will ever look the way we want to. But if we forget mirrors we may get somewhere close to it. Watching mirrors all the time just makes us look anxious and a little foolish."

"I suppose maybe you're right," said Leo with a sigh, "but—oh, well, that wasn't what I came to see you about anyway. I wanted to tell you that we're leaving early tomorrow—the circus, I mean—and to say good-bye. And to warn you about that Presto. Don't trust that wretched little white hopper any farther than you can push an elephant."

"Why, he seems like a harmless little chap," said Freddy.

"That's how he gets away with things," said Leo. "That's how Zing has got away with some pretty shady deals—using Presto to put up an innocent front for him."

"Are you sure of that?" Freddy asked. "I wouldn't trust Signor Zingo, but there can't be any harm in a white rabbit. Anyway, Zingo fired

Presto." And he told Leo about the missing hat, and how Presto had hired him to find it.

"OK," said the lion doubtfully. "You could be right, I suppose. But here's something I guess you haven't heard: the chief fired Zing tonight. Had a big row, so I hear, though I don't know what it was about; and Zing packed his stuff and moved out."

"He won't be going on with the show, then," said Freddy.

"He's taken a room at the hotel, I heard. Going to stay there the rest of the summer. So I'm warning you, Freddy—keep an eye peeled for trouble. . . . Well, I must get going. Lots to do before I go to bed. Good-bye, old pig." He whacked Freddy on the back with a huge paw, and by the time the pig had got his breath back the lion was gone.

Nothing much happened during the next few days. A number of hats were reported by Mr. Pomeroy as having been seen in the countryside northwest of Centerboro, but upon investigation turned out to be old discarded soft hats or derbies. No tall silk hats were found. Freddy worked hard at his magic lessons. With Presto's help he soon could do a dozen tricks skillfully enough to deceive an audience, and he began to talk about giving a public performance.

"I don't think you ought to yet, Freddy," said Mrs. Wiggins. She was the only one to whom he had shown the tricks, for he had very wisely decided not to perform them for any of his other friends until he was ready to give a show. "Everybody is awfully curious and interested," said the cow, "and they'll expect something pretty wonderful. And these tricks of yours—well, they're mysterious as anything, but they're all small ones, if you know what I mean—with coins and handkerchiefs and eggs and things. What you need is one real big splashy trick to finish up with. Like sawing a girl in two, for instance."

"Could you show me how to do that, Presto?" Freddy asked.

"Mrs. Wiggins is right, as always," said the rabbit, "and I can show you easily. But may I suggest something smaller—a dog, perhaps. Or a cat. Something with a long tail is preferable."

Freddy wanted to know why and Presto told him how the trick was done. And then all three of them went up into the loft over the barn, where there were tools and a work bench, and spent the rest of the day building the necessary apparatus.

But finding an animal who was willing to be sawed in two wasn't so easy. Georgie, the little brown dog, declined with thanks. "I'm very happy just as I am, Freddy," he said. "I can't see any advantage in being bisected. How'd I control my hind legs and my tail if I was running around in two sections?"

"We don't really saw you in two, of course," said the pig, who didn't want to reveal how the trick was done unless he first had Georgie's consent.

"You're darned right you don't," said the dog. "If you give a show, you'll see me there, but you won't saw me there." And he began to laugh. Freddy tried to argue, but Georgie was laughing so hard at his own wit that he wouldn't listen, and Freddy at last left him.

But everywhere the answer was the same. Nobody wanted to be sawed in two.

That evening Jinx dropped in to see Freddy. Jinx had been one of the first ones asked, and had refused with even more indignation than the others. But like all cats, he was curious, and wanted to know more about it. So Freddy, first binding him to secrecy, explained how the trick was done.

"Oh," said the cat. "Why didn't you say so in

the first place? Sure, I'll do it. But we'll have to wait till Minx gets here next week. She's coming to spend the rest of the summer with me."

Minx was Jinx's sister. She was a great traveler, had been abroad several times, and was always on the go. She never stayed very long in any one place. I guess maybe that was because nobody could stand her around for very long, for she was one of those people who always go you one better. If you had just been sick, she had just been sicker. If you had had a terrible experience, she had had the same one, only worse. Whatever you told her, the same thing had happened to her, only more so.

So Freddy agreed to wait. For a performance that ended up with sawing a cat in two would be something pretty special. Perhaps, Freddy thought, too special to be given just for the barn-yard animals and their friends. Perhaps he ought to hire a hall in Centerboro and give his show there. And he was thinking about this idea one afternoon when Mr. Pomeroy came in to tell him that a tall silk hat had been seen in the top of a tree on the eastern edge of the Big Woods. So Freddy and Presto went up to have a look at it.

## Chapter 5

The hat was caught in the crotch of a spruce about fifteen feet from the ground. Freddy and Presto peered up at it.

"It looks like the one, all right," said the rabbit. "How we going to get it?"

Freddy had on his magician's coat. He couldn't bear to be parted from it, so he wore it all the time, no matter how hot the weather was. He took out a rather grimy handkerchief and mopped his face all over. "We can shy sticks at it and knock it down," he said.

"And bust a hole in it," said Presto.

"Maybe we can get some help," Freddy said. He looked around. "There's a squirrel family lives around this section—Nibble, Dibble, Gribble—some such name. I can holler for them. Only the old man, he's kind of touchy, and if I call him by the wrong name, he might get mad. You know how people are. . . . Now what *is* that name?"

"Just call 'Ibble!" said Presto. "He won't notice you haven't put anything on the front of it."

So Freddy shouted: "Hey, Mr. Ibble!" several times, and at last an aged squirrel poked his head out of a hole in a hollow limb of a big beech tree and said crossly: "What do you want?"

"We'd like your help, if you'd be so kind," said Freddy politely, "in getting that hat."

"I daresay you would," said the squirrel. "Well, you won't get it!" And his head disappeared.

Freddy and Presto looked at each other. "H'm," said the pig after a moment. "Well, this is kind of a mean trick, but . . ." He felt in the pocket of his coat. "Hey," he called, "will you help us if I give you a nice fresh hen's egg?"

The squirrel popped out of the hole and

started down the tree. "Why didn't you say that in the first place?" he demanded testily. "Where's your egg?"

Freddy took it from his pocket and put it on the ground. "It's yours when you hand us that hat."

So the squirrel ran up the spruce and brought down the hat. But when he put out a paw to get hold of the egg it bounced away from him like a pingpong ball. For it was an egg that Freddy had pierced and blown for use in his magic work, and was of course nothing but an empty shell.

The squirrel was good and mad and I guess he had a right to be. He stamped and scolded and refused to listen to Freddy's promise to bring him two good eggs the following morning. "If that isn't a low-down pig trick, I never saw one!" he stormed. "Get out! Get out of my woods, you big hunk of fat pork! You—you—!" He sputtered and danced and screamed, and Freddy picked up the hat and, followed by Presto, started for home as fast as he could go.

"Well," he said, when they reached the pig pen, "you can get your job back now, Presto. But before you take the hat, I wish you'd show me the disappearing trick."

So Presto stood the hat on its crown on the floor. "Don't touch it," he said. "But look into it—look it all over. Just a hat, isn't it?"

Freddy examined it and peered inside it. It was lined with crinkled black silk, but it was plain there was nothing there but the lining.

Then Presto jumped into it.

"Cover the hat over with your handkerchief," he said. "And then say the magic words—'Presto-change-o!' And then take the handkerchief off."

So Freddy did. But when he looked in there was nothing there. Presto had vanished.

"My goodness!" said Freddy. "That's some trick! Presto! Presto, are you there?"

"Sure, I'm there," was the reply. "But I'm invisible."

Freddy was puzzled. He walked slowly around the hat, then he dodged quickly back around the other way, in case Presto was hiding behind it. Then he leaned over and peered in, and there was the crinkled black lining, but no rabbit. "Are you—you still there, Presto?" he said hesitatingly.

"Look, Freddy," said Presto's voice, and it certainly sounded as if it was within an inch of the pig's nose—"Look, it's like I told you: this

... *it bounced away from him like a ping pong ball.*

is the one trick I can't teach you, because it's real magic and not just tricks. I really make myself invisible, and if you stuck your nose out a little farther you could feel me, even though you can't see me. No, no; don't do it! If anybody touches me when I'm invisible it makes them invisible too, only they'd have to stay that way the rest of their lives, because they wouldn't know how to get visible again, and I can't teach that."

"You mean," said Freddy, "that you're transparent, like glass?"

"That's it."

"Golly!" Freddy exclaimed. "Wouldn't that be a swell thing in the detective business! Honestly, couldn't you teach me how, Presto?"

"Not possibly. I couldn't teach you how to disappear any more than I could teach you how to have white fur. Disappearing is hereditary; it runs in families, like big ears, or warts."

"Do warts run in families?" Freddy asked.

"I don't know," said Presto. "But you know what I mean—like six-toed cats. Well, how about putting your handkerchief over the hat again so I can appear?"

So Freddy did, and said: "Presto-change-o!" and took off the handkerchief and there sat the

rabbit in the hat. "Well," he said, "now I suppose you can take the hat to your boss and get
your job back."

"Oh, no hurry about that," Presto said. "I
like it here; nice to get a little quiet country life
after rushing around with a circus."

"That's all right," said Freddy. "I'd like to
keep on with the magic lessons for a while. But
you'll want a safe place to keep the hat. How
about the vaults of our bank? I'm the president
of the FIRST ANIMAL BANK, you know. Take it
down there now if you like."

So they went down to the bank, which was
in a shed beside the road, just below the gate.

## Chapter 6

"I'd really like to spend the rest of the summer here," said Presto as they walked along. "If the girls over at the cow barn are willing to let me stay on there. Nice comfortable place, but I must say, not very exciting. How do you ever stand them, Freddy? They're the stupidest creatures, even for cows, I ever met."

Freddy turned angrily on him. "Those cows are my friends, rabbit!" he said. "And even if they weren't—it's not a very nice thing to accept their hospitality and then talk about them behind their backs."

Presto was all apologies. "You misunderstood me, Freddy. I was just going to say: they're so nice and kind, you don't mind that they aren't clever. In fact, if they were clever, you wouldn't get half as fond of them as you do. I think . . ."

"All right, all right," Freddy interrupted, "let's just talk about something else." And as they had reached the bank, he took Presto in and introduced him to the two rabbits who were on guard at the trap door leading down to the vaults.

"Those rabbits aren't much protection," Presto said. "A robber could just walk in and knock them over and clean out the place."

"Oh, it's safe enough," said Freddy. He didn't tell Presto about the alarm bell. Just outside the bank hung a big iron bell that had once been the Bean's dinner bell. A cord fastened to the clapper led through a hole into the bank, and if danger threatened, all the guards had to do was pull the cord once, and the clang would bring every animal on the farm running to the defense of the bank.

So they went down into the vaults and put the silk hat in one of the underground rooms that the woodchucks had hollowed out when the bank was built. And then they went back to the pig pen and had another magic lesson.

But Freddy was worried. He was worried about the way Presto had spoken of the cows. "I thought he was pretty insincere," he said later to Jinx, "because he flatters everybody so outrageously; but I did think he was a gentleman. Now I'm not so sure."

"H'm," said Jinx, "it's funny about cows. They're what?—twenty, thirty times as big as I am, and you'd think they ought to be twenty times as smart. But you've got to admit it, Freddy, that Wogus and Wurzburger are a pair of pretty dull girls. Not Mrs. Wiggins; she's got the brains of the family, all right."

"Just the same, that Presto had no business making a crack like that. He'll bear watching."

Freddy was worried too about the hat. He was sure that Presto had really vanished. And at the same time he was sure that the rabbit had played some trick and hadn't really vanished at all.

It is funny how you can have two opinions in your head like that at the same time. It is as if one side of your head thought something was so, while the other side thinks it isn't so, and the two sides keep arguing with each other until you are almost crazy. The argument went on inside Freddy's head until he couldn't keep his mind on the tricks, and he sent Presto away and sat down and tried to write some poetry for the next issue of the Bean Home News. This is what he wrote:

*O give me a home*
*Where no buffaloes roam,*
*But the pigs and the porcupines play.*
*If it rains, we've the barn,*
*So we don't give a darn*
*When the skies are all cloudy and grey.*

*Home, home on the farm.*
*Where the corn and the canteloupes grow;*
*Where often is seen*
*Mr. William F. Bean,*
*And the—*

At this point the argument inside his head got so violent that he threw down his pencil and said: "Bosh!" And when the song came out in the paper it was still unfinished. But Freddy put a note underneath it that said: "I was too busy this week to finish this. So if you want to sing it, you'll have to write the last line yourselves. There are lots of rhymes: blow, glow, slow, flow, toe, buffalo, etc."

"If I keep on arguing with myself like this," Freddy decided, "I will go crazy, and they will have to tie me up and feed me with a spoon. I guess I'll go up and see old Whibley."

Old Whibley lived up in the woods and he was pretty cross, even for an owl. But he never refused his advice when Freddy asked for it, although he always made it plain that he considered the pig a great nuisance.

"You again!" he said grumpily, when he had come to the door of his nest. "Well, been making a fool of yourself, I suppose. Come, come; what is it? I haven't got all day."

So Freddy told him about Presto's hat trick and the struggle it had aroused in his own mind.

"Pshaw!" said the owl. "Simple enough. All depends on what you believe. If you believe in magic, then it was magic and that's all there is to it. If you don't believe in magic, then it was a trick, and anybody can do it."

"Well, I—I don't believe in magic, really," said Freddy.

"More fool you," said the owl. "But it makes our problem simpler. Now the rabbit—did he ever disappear except when he was in the hat?"

*"You again!" he said grumpily.*

Freddy said: "No, I think he has to have the hat."

"Look!" said Old Whibley impatiently. "Look, pig;" and he bit the words off even shorter than usual as if he was holding back his irritation with a great effort—"you have rabbit and hat. Rabbit gets in hat. Rabbit disappears. Is it magic?"

"N-no, I don't think so."

"Then it's the hat. A trick hat. Maybe little door in hat—rabbit crawled out and hid behind it."

"But I walked all around it," said Freddy.

"Then he was inside."

"But I looked. He wasn't there."

Old Whibley gave an exasperated hoot. "You call yourself a detective!" he said. "Got a big reputation—master of disguises. But can't figure out how a white rabbit can hide in a black hat. Go on back home, you're wasting my time."

"Oh, but please!" said Freddy, as the owl started back into his hole. "Won't you please tell me what you think?"

"With pleasure," said Whibley. "Think you're a numbskull," and disappeared.

Freddy knew there was no more to be got out of him, and he trudged back home. But on the way he did some thinking, and instead of going to the pig pen he went down to the bank, dismissed the guards, and brought the hat up from the vault and set it on the floor. Then he peered inside. "Yes," he thought, "if Presto had had something black to cover himself with I couldn't have seen him. But there's nothing in there—nothing but that crinkled black silk lining." He reached in and felt around the inside. No, there was nothing loose; the lining was tight all around the inside. But wait a minute! It gave when he pushed up into the crown. Was there a space there?

He took the hat over to the window. And then he saw how the trick had been done. "My good gracious!" he said. "It's got a false bottom! Or a false top, I guess you'd call it. That darned Presto!" For there was a space a good two and a half inches deep between the top of the hat and the silk lining. When you looked into it it was so black inside that you didn't notice that it wasn't as deep as it should have been. And all Presto had done was push his nose through the circular elastic that held the top lining together in the middle, and then crawl into the space. The elastic pulled the lining together, and there was an apparently empty hat.

Freddy put the hat back in the vault and went out to look for Presto to tell him about his discovery. But the more he thought about it, the more he thought he'd keep it to himself for a while. Anyway, Presto wasn't anywhere around. And so as it was still early in the day, he thought he would trot down to Centerboro and see what he could do about renting a hall for his performance.

## Chapter 7

A pig in a rather loud checked sports coat trudging along the highway is an unusual sight. Of course the local people all knew Freddy, and they just waved as they drove by. But there were a lot of tourists on the road, and they stared and shouted, and one old lady from California who was going back home after visiting her grandson in Schenectady fainted dead away, and her car ran into the ditch. Freddy helped her get it back on the road, and she was so pleased with his kindness and good manners and with several tricks he performed for her, that she decided to sell her house in California and buy a place in Centerboro and live there. She did, too. Her name is Mrs. Hattie Bland, and she lives in that little white house opposite Mrs. Underdunk's.

Freddy went to see Mr. Muszkiski, the manager of the movie theatre, and arranged to rent the theatre next Tuesday night for his magic show. Because the theatre was always dark Tuesday evening, and Mr. Muszkiski was glad to get a little money for it. Then Freddy went down to see Mr. Dimsey, who printed the Bean Home News, and had some signs made.

---

## PROFESSOR FREDERICO
### THE WORLD-FAMOUS MAGICIAN

Presents a program of tricks, sleight of hand, and mystifications.

**Astounding! Breath-taking! Incredible!**

## SPECIAL ATTRACTION:
### A CAT WILL BE SAWED IN TWO!

Tuesday, Aug. 25th        8 P.M. sharp

*People: 50¢     Children and animals: 25¢*

---

When his business was done, Freddy strolled down Main Street, but he hadn't gone far when a hand fell on his shoulder and he turned to see a tall man with a straggly moustache who wore no coat or necktie, and had a silver star pinned to his vest. It was his friend the sheriff.

"Is this a pinch?" Freddy asked.

The sheriff grinned. "You can call it that," he said. "You're just the party I wanted to contact, as they say in the business world. Come on over to the jail."

The prisoners were playing ball on the diamond the sheriff had laid out for them back of the jail, and besides the two teams there was quite a crowd in the bleachers.

"Crime on the up-swing?" Freddy inquired, as they stopped to look.

"Had quite a few robberies lately," said the sheriff. "Of course, we've been able to have two full teams all this last year, but it's nice to have some onlookers."

"You lost your best pitcher last spring, didn't you?" Freddy asked.

"Red Mike? Yes, his sentence expired, and he had to go out. But Mike's a good guy, and he didn't want to let us down. Day he got out, he went up to Judge Willey's and stole a hen, and the judge gave him three months—just enough to finish out the ball season."

After a while they went into the office and the sheriff said seriously: "Freddy, there's been a robbery in the jail." He looked at the pig unhappily. "Can't understand it; such a thing has never happened before in all my years as sheriff. My boys here are better behaved and honester than most of the folks outside, and I know that for a fact."

Freddy could never quite understand the sheriff's attitude toward his prisoners. He said impatiently: "How can you say that? They're criminals, aren't they? How about Red Mike, who stole a hen as soon as he got out?"

"Pshaw!" said the sheriff; "he didn't want that hen. He just did it so he could get back in jail. He likes it here."

"Well, well," said Freddy, "I suppose you want me to detect the thief. What was stolen?"

"A pie."

"What kind of pie?"

"What in tunket difference does it make?" said the sheriff. "Pie's a pie, ain't it?"

"Not to a detective," said Freddy. "You take a crime like this, sheriff, and it looks insoluble, doesn't it? Anybody might have taken the pie. But suppose it's a pieplant pie. Maybe there's some of the prisoners don't like pieplant. So your case narrows down, do you see? And the more facts you get, the more it narrows, until at last you point your finger at one man, and say: 'There's the thief.' "

The sheriff said: "Yeah," and went out to see the cook. "It was a blueberry pie," he said when he came back, "and all the boys like blueberry. So where does that narrow you down to?"

"You'd be surprised," said Freddy. "How long ago was it stolen?"

"Not more'n an hour."

"OK," said Freddy. "You get all the prisoners lined up out there—the game seems to be over. Tell 'em I want to show 'em a trick."

So the sheriff called the prisoners together and had them line up out by the baseball diamond, and Freddy stood out in front of them and did one or two simple tricks. "Now gentlemen," he said, "I have a special trick here which has never before been performed publicly. If you will be so good as all to stick out your tongues—no, not at the sheriff, just at me. Good! Good! Just a little farther. Ah, thank you, gentlemen." He walked down the line. All the tongues were pink except that of a prisoner called Louie the Lout. His was blue. Freddy touched him on the shoulder. "Here's your thief, sheriff."

"Now, why couldn't I have thought of that!" said the sheriff admiringly. "Well, Louie, I'm disappointed in you. I guess you'd better go up to your room. I'll see you later. Freddy, come along back into the office."

"Well, what are you going to do with Louie?" Freddy asked.

"I guess," said the sheriff, "he'll have to go. Can't have a thief in my jail."

"My goodness," Freddy said, "most of 'em are here because they're thieves, aren't they?"

The sheriff admitted that was so. "But just the same," he said—"oh, you know what it is, Freddy. It's kind of hard to explain."

"Harder than about the pies," said the pig. "Yes, but I do know what you mean. He's being punished for being a thief by being put in jail. But it's against the rules, kind of, for him to go on being a thief while he's being punished."

"That's right. If he's allowed to go on stealing here, what becomes of the punishment?"

Freddy grinned. "What becomes of it anyway in this jail?"

"You tell me," said the sheriff. "Oh, well, it

*All tongues were pink except . . .*

keeps 'em out of mischief. How about splitting one of those other pies before you start back?"

On Tuesday morning Freddy hitched Hank up to the old phaeton, into which he loaded all his magic paraphernalia, and then he and Jinx and Minx and Presto got in and drove to Centerboro. Minx had just come in from the West Coast the night before on a fast freight, and she had kept Jinx up all night telling him about her experiences. In spite of that, she was as fresh as ever, and she chattered and bragged until Freddy, who wanted a little peace and quiet to plan out that evening's performance, asked her if she didn't think she ought to sit back and rest a while.

"Mercy, no; I'm not tired!" she said. "And I know how anxious you are to hear about all my wonderful experiences! Hollywood—ah, what a marvelous place, Freddy! You know I was in the movies last winter. I was selected from forty others to play opposite Gregory Peck in one of the big scenes in his new picture. Such a charming man! I sat on his lap and he scratched my ears."

"Wish he'd pulled out your tongue," Jinx grumbled.

Minx gave an amused little mew. "That's my loving brother speaking, Freddy. And yet you *are* proud of me, aren't you, Jinxie?—in spite of the awful things you say."

Jinx gave an exasperated snarl. "Don't call me *Jinxie!*" he said. He glared at her for a moment, then jumped over into the back seat and got into the box he was to be sawed in two in and shut the lid.

"Isn't he cute?" said Minx indulgently. "You know, he's really awfully fond of me, only he just hates to let anyone see it."

"Yeah," Freddy said. "If he was any fonder of you he'd probably cut your throat."

"Oh, *you!*" Minx tapped him playfully on his shoulder with her paw. And then she went on with anecdotes of her brother's cuteness when he was a kitten that made Jinx squirm inside the box almost as much as if he was really being sawed in two.

When they reached the movie theatre, and had unloaded the stuff and carried it back onto the stage, and Minx had gone out to take a walk and look over the town, Freddy said: "You know, Jinx, I'd forgotten what a conversationalist your sister is."

"Conversationalist!" the cat exclaimed. "You won't hurt my feelings if you say what you really mean."

"Well, she is kind of a nuisance," Freddy said. "But we need her help for the magic performance. And you'll admit it was nice of her to be so willing to give it."

"Willing?" Jinx said. "To get out on a stage in front of a lot of people? She'd claw her best friend's eyes out for the chance. And watch out, Freddy—she'll steal the show if you aren't careful." He sighed deeply. "And I've got her on my hands for a week!"

"You know," said Freddy, "I've got an idea. Yes, sir, I believe it will work. I believe I can figure out a scheme to keep her from saying a word all week."

"If you can do that," said the cat, "you're some magician all right. Only I don't see how . . ."

But Freddy wouldn't tell him how. "You leave it to me," he said.

Freddy and Presto and Jinx worked all day to get the stage set for the show, and Freddy put on his magician's coat and rehearsed his tricks several times to be sure that they went smoothly. At noon they went to Dixon's Diner and had lunch. Judge Willey came in just as they were leaving.

The judge shook hands with Jinx, and with Freddy, whom he addressed as "my learned friend," and then Presto was introduced to him. He looked sharply at the rabbit. "Ah yes, the conjuror's rabbit," he said. "And how is the good Signor Zingo?"

"I really don't know, sir," said Presto. "We —we had a disagreement; we don't see each other any more."

"That's odd," said the judge. "Haven't you called on him recently at the hotel? I saw you coming out through the lobby—let me see, a week ago yesterday, and I naturally assumed you'd been to see him."

"What's that?" Freddy asked, turning to frown at the rabbit. "That was the day we found the hat, and you disappeared in the afternoon."

"It wasn't me," said Presto. "Probably he's advertised that he wants to hire another rabbit to take my place, and this was an applicant for the job."

"Possibly," said the judge. He looked hard at Freddy and gave his head a slight shake which said plainly: "No, it was this rabbit all right." Then he said good afternoon and went on.

Freddy was disturbed. If Presto was seeing Zingo on the sly, there was something very queer going on. Perhaps Signor Zingo had never really fired the rabbit at all; perhaps . . . But no use thinking about it now. The show, said Freddy to himself like a good trouper, must go on.

## Chapter 8

And on it went. Presto had suggested that it might be a good idea if, before the curtain went up, he were to come out and make a short speech, introducing Professor Frederico, and giving some facts about how famous he was and so on. He said it was customary at such performances, and Freddy said that if it was customary, then it was the thing to do. So at eight o'clock sharp, Presto hopped out in front of the curtain and addressed the audience.

Freddy didn't listen very attentively to the

speech. He was peeking at the audience through
a hole in the curtain. The lights were still on
of course in the body of the house, and he could
see that every seat was taken, and Mr. Muszkiski was setting up folding chairs in the aisles
for latecomers who were still straggling in. In
the middle of the front row were Mr. and Mrs.
Bean, in their best clothes, looking very proud
and pleased; and beside them were all the small
animals, who of course would not be able to see
anything if they had seats farther back. Charles
and Henrietta were there, and Georgie, and
Robert, the collie, and Alice and Emma, the
two ducks, with their Uncle Wesley, and Sniffy
Wilson, the skunk, with his family, and a dozen
others. And in the crowded rows behind them
Freddy picked out one by one the faces of friends.
Everybody was there: Judge Willey and the
sheriff, and Mr. Weezer and Mrs. Peppercorn
and Dr. Winterpool and Mr. Beller and Freddy's
old friend, Mrs. Winfield Church. And in the
back seats were the larger animals: the three
cows and Peter, the bear, and his cousins, and
Hank, as well as a number of friends from neigh-
boring farms. It would take ten pages to list all
the faces that Freddy recognized, to say nothing
of strangers.

Freddy was too old a hand at public appearances to be bothered by stage fright. But he had never done his tricks before an audience. He had practiced them until he felt that they were about perfect, but only before a looking glass, with Presto to make suggestions. And if he slipped up on just one of them . . .

"Hey!" said Jinx, who was standing beside him. "Listen—listen to that rabbit! You've got to do something, Freddy—quick!"

"And so, ladies and gentlemen," Presto was saying, "in view of the astounding nature of his feats, and to prove to you that they are really magic and not mere tricks, Professor Frederico offers to anyone who can duplicate, or even explain any one of them a prize of five dollars in cash. Five dollars, ladies, gentlemen and animals, for each and every . . ."

"O lordy, lordy," Freddy said, "what is the matter with the idiot!" He tugged at the bottom of the heavy curtain, trying to lift it so he could get out in front and stop the rabbit, who was now repeating the offer.

"Have to go around," said Jinx. "You go that way and I'll go this, and boy, what I'll do to that lop-eared pest—"

"And now, ladies and gentlemen," Presto

was saying, "I introduce to you that master of magic, mystification and mummery, that prince of prestidigitators, that dauntless detective, that peerless poetic pig, Professor Frederico."

And at that moment Freddy did indeed appear. He came tearing across the front of the stage from one side, and Jinx came bounding from the other. Presto's ears went down with a snap; he gave a terrified squeal and leaped right over the footlights into the audience, and went skittering and scrambling up under people's feet towards the door.

"Stop that animal!" Freddy shouted.

Everybody laughed and applauded, for of course they thought it was all part of the show. And then: "We've got him!" somebody called, and Peter came down the aisle holding the struggling Presto in one huge paw.

"Just take charge of him till the show's over, will you, Peter?" Freddy said. Then he motioned for the lights in the house to go down and the curtain to go up.

Jinx had gone back and was standing with his forelegs folded beside the sawing-in-two box, in the correct position for a magician's assistant. Freddy, as he smiled and bowed, was thinking hard. How could he withdraw the dreadful offer

*He gave a terrified squeal and leaped right over the footlights. . . .*

that Presto had made? It would make a terribly bad impression, and even though probably nobody in the audience had any hope of exposing one of the tricks, everybody would feel disappointed and let down.

And then Freddy saw that he would have to let the offer stand. He was pretty sure to lose some money on it, but a lot of tickets had been sold at the box office and enough money had been taken in over and above the rent of the theatre and other expenses to give him a nice profit. And so without saying anything he started his performance.

Everything went well at first. He made coins and other small objects disappear and he made a glass go through a solid table, and did one or two other tricks which were heartily applauded.

Then he took off his silk hat and put it down on the stage with the brim up close to the footlights. This of course was his own silk hat which you may remember he had borrowed from a scarecrow in the course of some detective work a year or so before. He took out a handkerchief and waved it around to show that it had nothing in it. "My invisible hen," he said, "will now lay an egg for you in my hat. Come, Mabel!"

"Praaa*aawk*! Kut, kut, kut, kut," said the

invisible hen. Freddy said afterwards that imitating a hen was the hardest part of the trick.

"Thank you, Mabel; I knew you'd oblige," he said. He folded the handkerchief around one trotter, held it as if the hen was sitting on it, shook it gently, and an egg dropped out into the hat.

The audience clapped, and Henrietta, who was naturally much interested, fluttered up and perched on the edge of the stage. "Let me see that egg," she said.

"Now you lay one, Henrietta," Sniffy Wilson called. But Freddy lifted up the handkerchief and shoved the hat towards her.

Henrietta gave a cluck of amazement. "There's no egg here!"

"Invisible hens naturally lay invisible eggs," said Freddy. "But kindly resume your seat and I will have Mabel lay another one."

"Let me try, Professor," said a voice, and down the aisle came Signor Zingo in his red-lined cape, with a superior smile on his thin lips.

"Oh, dear!" said Freddy to himself. "Here goes five bucks! So that's what Presto was up to." But he put as good a face upon it as possible. He shook hands with Signor Zingo, and said: "Welcome! I am very pleased to have so distinguished a colleague on the same platform with me."

"You won't be pleased when I get through with you," the magician murmured; then he smiled and said: "Thank you, my friend. You are very gracious. May I have that handkerchief?" And when Freddy resigned it to him he held it up by the corners. And everyone saw that suspended from the middle of the upper side by a thread was an egg. But of course it was only a shell, for Freddy had pierced it at both ends and then blown out the contents.

"The trick is done in this way," he said. "When you show the handkerchief, the egg is in your hand. You fold the handkerchief over the egg, shake it, and the egg drops out. Then you pull it back into the handkerchief and show that the hat is empty. Have I earned my five dollars?"

"Mrs. Wiggins," Freddy called, "pay Signor Zingo five dollars when he leaves."

The magician showed his teeth in a malicious smile, and swept a deep bow. "Thank you, Professor. And now may I demonstrate *my* invisible hen?" He folded the handkerchief, knelt beside the hat, and one after another six eggs dropped into it. He took them out and laid them on the stage. "And now Professor Frederico will explain that trick, and I will pay him back his five dollars, and another five to go with it."

Well, of course Freddy knew that the eggs had been brought out from some secret pocket in Zingo's clothing, but it was quite impossible for him to explain the trick. He looked out at the audience. The faces that he could see looked pleased and interested; evidently they still thought all this was part of the show and arranged for beforehand.

But Zingo had underestimated the pig's resourcefulness. Freddy smiled and said: "Thank you, Signor Zingo. But I prefer not to explain it. What I would like to explain however, ladies and gentlemen, in case you think my refusal is due to ignorance, is that no reputable magician will ever disclose to the public how his, or any other magician's tricks are done. The secrets of the profession are carefully and jealously guarded. You will understand why. Once you explain the tricks, there is nothing to perform. No respectable magician will ever disclose them, for he is taking away his own livelihood and that of his colleagues, throwing dozens of magicians out of work, and destroying an honorable profession which has given millions of people a great deal of pleasure.

"And now, sir," he said, turning to Zingo, "if you will step down the performance will go on."

The audience, which had at first thought that Signor Zingo had really come up to help Freddy, began to catch on to what he was up to, and there was a roar of applause, and shouts of "Good old Freddy!" "Keep it up, pig; we're with you!" And Peter the bear lumbered down the aisle, with Presto still clutched in his paw, and said: "Want me to show you how I make a magician disappear?"

But Freddy shook his head. "No. We'll just go on."

Signor Zingo was furious. To be accused of breaking the unwritten laws of his profession was a serious charge. But he had had too much stage experience to lose his temper openly. He held up a hand and the uproar died down. "Professor Frederico is quite correct," he said. "But he failed to draw the distinction between the very simple and rather childish tricks which everyone can do, and the really difficult feats which only a few top flight magicians have the secret of. There are books on simple magic; this hen trick is in all of them, and I have therefore disclosed no secret. But as for the difficult tricks —well, let me show you one."

"Excuse me," said Freddy, who was getting good and mad, "but is this your show or mine? If it's yours, I'll step down and you go on."

Zingo looked out at the audience. He realized that they were not with him. There was a sprinkling of strangers, who looked pleased and expectant, as if they would be glad to have him take over, but the majority glared angrily at him. Mr. Bean's whiskers were fluttering, and it was plain that he was saying uncomplimentary things behind them, and Sniffy Wilson had beckoned to his family and they had got up and started towards the gangway that led up to the stage.

The evening might have been pleasanter in the end if Zingo had taken over the stage. The animals would have thrown him out and Freddy's show would have gone on. But the magician didn't really want to steal the show, even though he felt sure that he could swing the audience over to his side. He had other plans for the evening. So he bowed to Freddy and said:

"I beg your pardon, sir. I will step down at

once." Then he paused. "But your offer still stands, of course?"

"Of course!" Freddy snapped.

So Signor Zingo went back to his seat in the rear of the hall and the show went on.

## Chapter 9

Of course Freddy had intended to have both Presto and Jinx with him on the stage, as assistants. The rabbit, who knew all the tricks, would hand him things at the right moment and attract the audience's attention when he was doing something he didn't want them to see, and would be a big help. But with only Jinx to help him, Freddy knew that things wouldn't go as well. And of course they didn't.

But although he made a lot of mistakes, Jinx turned out to be a better assistant than the rabbit, for he overacted and clowned and behaved so outrageously that the audience was delighted with him. When Freddy did a trick, Jinx would be so astonished that he would fall over backward in a faint, or he would screech and run right up the scenery; and when Freddy held out something for him to take, he would crouch, lashing his tail and snarling, and then make a wild leap for it. As Mrs. Bean said afterwards to Mr. Bean: "That cat is a whole show in himself. And I'm going to give him half a pint of cream when we get home, and don't you try to stop me, Mr. B.!"

But Signor Zingo was still there. After about every other trick he would come up on the stage and explain how it was done, and then do it better, and Freddy would have to promise him another five dollars. By the time the show was half over he was sixty dollars ahead—and that was already as much as Freddy figured he was going to make out of the performance.

The audience was by now really hostile to the magician. They hooted and hissed when he walked down the aisle, and Judge Willey, who had an end seat, even stuck his foot out and tripped him up once when he was coming back from the stage. But Freddy came to Signor Zingo's assistance. He knew that, whatever it cost, he had to be a good sport and stick to the offer that had been made in his name. So he hammered on the table and called for silence. "Signor Zingo is quite within his rights," he shouted. "I must ask you to give him your attention."

Fortunately, Freddy had thought up some tricks which Zingo couldn't duplicate. He had had the bright idea of getting the four mice who lived in the Bean kitchen to help him. So he had Eek in one inside pocket and Eeny in the other, and Quik and Cousin Augustus had what you might call roving commissions—that is, they ran around Freddy under his coat and brought out things and pulled them out of sight and generally helped out. One of the mouse tricks was when Freddy stood perfectly still in the center of the stage while Mr. Beller played the Star Spangled Banner on the piano, and then out of Freddy's pockets would come four little American flags on sticks which would be waved in time to the music. Another was one that Freddy called the "Shower of Gold." He had a lot of nickels in his pockets that he had painted with radiator paint so they looked like five-dollar gold pieces. He went down into the audience and stood in the center aisle, and then

while two people held his arms, the mice threw
out the nickels, which flashed and jingled, and
it did indeed look as if Freddy's pockets were
spouting gold pieces. A lot of the audience got
right down on the floor and scrambled for them,
and even Mr. Weezer, the president of the Centerboro Bank, got his head caught under his
seat while he was hunting for one, and had to
be pulled out by the heels.

Signor Zingo didn't come forward after that
trick, and Freddy said: "To anyone who can
explain that trick I offer twenty dollars." He
paused. "Well, Signor Zingo," he said, "how
about it? I can't believe it is your modesty that
holds you back. Can it be ignorance?"

"Pooh," said the magician from the back of
the hall, "any fool can do that trick."

"Come on up and prove it then," said Freddy,
"by doing it yourself."

The audience giggled, and Zingo lost his
temper. "You stupid fat lummox!" he shouted.
"Call me a fool, will you! Why, you—" But he
didn't say any more for a huge paw fell on his
shoulder and a deep bear's voice growled menacingly in his ear. He sat down quickly.

Mr. Bean had caught sight of a mouse's paw
holding one of the little flags in the other trick,

and he had a pretty good idea what was going on. He nudged Mrs. Bean. "Here's your chance to make twenty dollars," he whispered.

But Mrs. Bean just smiled. She wouldn't have exposed the trick for ten times the amount. And of course, neither would Mr. Bean.

At last Freddy announced that he was about to do the most mysterious feat of the evening. He was going to saw a cat in two and put him together again. He called for two volunteers from the audience to assist him.

"Go on up, Mr. B., and help him," Mrs Bean whispered.

But Mr. Bean said no. "Folks know he's my pig," he said. "They'll think I'm a confederate."

So at last Mr. Weezer and Judge Willey went up, and Freddy had them carry a box about eighteen inches long and eight inches high from the back of the stage and put it on two chairs, so that the middle of the box was over the space between the chairs. He opened the box and had Jinx jump in, then he closed the lid and came forward and addressed the audience.

"Ladies and gentlemen," he said, "you have seen a live cat jump into this box. I will now ask him to put his head and forepaws out of one end of the box, and his tail and hind paws out of the other." And immediately a black head and forepaws came out through holes in one end of the box, and a black tail and hind paws out of holes at the other.

"You see now," Freddy went on, "that the cat is actually in the box, and if it is sawed in two the cat will be in two pieces. And now, to show that there is no deception, I will ask Mr. Weezer to steady the box while Judge Willey takes this saw and saws right down through box and cat and . . ."

"Stop!" called old Mrs. Peppercorn, jumping up from her seat. "I won't permit it!" She turned to face the audience. "What kind of people are you, to sit there with grins on your faces while this wretched pig murders a cat? It's cruelty to animals of the worst kind. Sheriff, I call on you to arrest this animal."

"Why, ma'am," drawled the sheriff, "I can't see he's hurt the cat any yet. Critter seems real happy." And Freddy said: "I assure you, ma'am, if I were not perfectly certain that I could put him together again, I wouldn't attempt this trick. How about it, Jinx?"

"Sure," said Jinx, twisting around and grinning at the audience. "Bring on your saws! The duller they are, the better I like 'em."

"Well, maybe you can fool that cat into letting you do it—he don't seem like a very smart animal," said Mrs. Peppercorn, "but you can't make me believe you'll ever get him together again. Judge Willey, I'm ashamed of you, lending yourself to such a wicked performance. And if you don't stop at once, I'm going to go out and call up the state troopers."

Freddy came forward. "Would you just step down here a moment, ma'am?" he said, and as she came down to the stage he knelt and whispered in her ear.

The audience watched them intently. As Freddy talked, they saw Mrs. Peppercorn's narrow shoulders begin to shake. Then fizzing sounds came from her, and her friends knew that she was laughing, although those who didn't know her might have supposed that she was about to explode. Then suddenly she turned, holding one hand over her mouth, and hurried back up the aisle to her seat.

A good many people in the audience, even those who were not personal friends of the victim, had been disturbed about the business. Those who had been to the circus and seen a girl sawed in two knew that it was only a trick, but there were some who agreed with Mrs. Peppercorn, and Mrs. Weezer, who sat next to her, said: "Is it really all right? What did he tell you?"

But all Mrs. Peppercorn would say, between chuckles, was that it was all right: Freddy had a sawing-in-two license, and the law couldn't touch him.

Now of course the way the trick was worked was this: when Jinx had jumped into the box, Minx was already in it, unknown to the audience, and while it was Jinx's head and forepaws that came out through the holes in one end of the box, it was Minx's tail and hind paws that appeared through the holes in the other end. And the saw went right down between the two cats.

Jinx put on a good show while the judge sawed him in two. He wriggled and screeched at first, but when he saw that that was too much for the audience, he stopped pretending that he was being hurt, and began to shriek with laughter, shouting that Judge Willey was tickling him. And the box was sawed quite through, and Freddy pulled the chairs an inch or so apart, so that people could see right between the two halves of the box, each of which apparently contained half of Jinx.

*. . . it did look sort of awful.*

Then Freddy turned the chairs so that the ends of the box faced the audience, and now there were evidently two boxes, with a head and forepaws sticking out of one, and a tail and hind-paws sticking out of the other, and even those who knew it was only a trick gasped, for it did look sort of awful.

"And now, ladies and gentlemen," Freddy said, "I will put my friend together again." He moved the chairs around, shoved the box together as it had been at first, opened the lid, the head, tail and paws disappeared from the ends and out jumped Jinx, all in one piece.

The applause beat upon Freddy's ears like the roar of a mighty ocean—at least that was how he expressed it himself later; and although he had never seen the ocean, except in a flat calm on that famous trip to Florida, I guess he was about right. He bowed and bowed again, and after the curtain went down, it had to be pulled up again five times so that he could bow some more. And then it went down for good and the show was over.

Freddy came down from the stage and hurried out through the crowd to the ticket booth, stopping briefly to receive the congratulations of friends.

"Well," he said to Mrs. Wiggins, "how did we come out?"

Mrs. Wiggins didn't say anything. She pushed a little piece of paper towards him. On it was written:

## Receipts

| | |
|---|---|
| 50¢ tickets | $118. |
| 25¢ tickets | 154.75 |
| | $172.75 |

## Expenditures

| | |
|---|---|
| Rent of theatre | $ 50. |
| Other expenses | 21.42 |
| Paid Signor Zingo | 130. |
| | $201.42 |

"You still owe Zingo $28.67."

"H'm," said Freddy, "we didn't do so well."

Mrs. Wiggins just looked at him, and two large tears rolled out of her eyes and splashed on the little counter in front of her.

Freddy was alarmed. It was pretty nice of Mrs. Wiggins to feel so badly on his account, but he knew that if she once really got started crying, she would alarm the whole town. She often said herself that when she was really unhappy she didn't care who knew it, and it was a good thing she didn't, for she bawled so that nobody within two miles could fail to hear her. And it was the same when she laughed. Freddy had seen birds shaken right out of trees when somebody told Mrs. Wiggins a joke.

So now he said sharply: "Stop it! Stop it at once! Good gracious, I've got plenty of money that I made last year with the circus. I can pay Zingo and never feel it."

"But I feel it, Freddy," she sniffed. "I feel it terribly. All your hard work, and then—"

"Nonsense!" said the pig. "We'll get Zingo yet; don't you worry about that. And by the way, when did he leave? He wasn't in the house during the sawing-in-two trick, was he?"

"He left just as you started it. Came out for his money. I gave him what there was, and he said he'd expect the rest by noon tomorrow."

"He'll get it," Freddy said. "I didn't think he'd care to expose that trick, since he does the same one himself. Well, come on. We'll let Mr. Muszkiski lock up and go home."

The Beans, with the smaller animals, had gone on ahead in the phaeton, and as soon as he could get away from the lobby, where a number of people were still waiting to thank him for his fine show, Freddy and the cows set out for home. With them were the two cats, and Peter, who still had the terrified Presto clutched in one big paw.

Nothing much was said on the way home. They were all rather depressed. When they came to the beginning of the Bean farm, Peter said: "Well, I turn off here to go up to the woods. What do you want done with this rabbit, Freddy?"

"Oh, please, Mr. Freddy," Presto wailed, "won't you please let me go? I didn't want to make that speech, but Signor Zingo made me —he said he'd—well, he'd do awful things to me if I didn't."

"I don't believe he said anything of the kind," Freddy replied. "I think you've been in with him all the time. You went to see him at the hotel. I don't believe he ever fired you in the first place. How about telling us the truth? We might let you go if you tell us the whole thing."

"Oh dear!" the rabbit whimpered. "I would if—Oh I feel so sick!" And his head waggled from side to side and then fell limply forward as if all the stiffness had gone out of his neck.

"Oh, the poor little fellow!" said Mrs. Wogus, and Mrs. Würzburger said: "Don't tease him any more, Freddy. I'm sure he didn't mean to do any harm."

"Poor little nothing!" said Freddy. "Hang on to him, Peter." For he saw that the rabbit was pretending to be sick so that Peter would set him down.

"You bet I'll hang on," said the bear, "and you watch yourself, rabbit."

"But my stomach is upset," Presto moaned.

"Upset, eh? We can fix that," said Peter, and took the rabbit in both paws and shook him hard. "See if we can't get it right side up again," he said. "That feel better?"

"Oh, yes! Please! Please, it's all right; I'm not sick any more."

"How curious!" said Minx. "I remember once when I was crossing on the Queen Mary I cured a friend of seasickness by—"

"Shut up, sis!" said Jinx sharply. "And you too," he added, turning on Mrs. Wogus and Mrs. Wurzburger, who were making shocked and sympathetic noises in the background. "Go on, Freddy; make him come clean."

Presto was now thoroughly scared, and he said: "I'll talk. I'll talk if you'll just let me go."

He probably didn't intend to tell very much of the truth, but Freddy was a shrewd and ex-

perienced questioner, and bit by bit the story
came out. At the circus, when Mr. Boomschmidt had told Signor Zingo who Freddy was,
the magician had started to turn back to ask
Freddy to find the hat that had blown away in
the storm. But he had just had a quarrel with
Freddy, and didn't believe that the pig would
take on any job for him. So he got Presto to
do it. He had had the rabbit make up the story
about being fired, for he felt that Freddy's sympathy for a poor unemployed rabbit would in-
duce him to organize a search for the hat. And
of course that was the way it worked out.

Presto confessed that he had visited the magician several times and reported progress.
Zingo knew that the hat had been found and
was in the bank vault.

"Well then," said Freddy, "you can go down
to Zingo, and tell him that when he pays my
bill for services rendered in finding the hat, he
can have it. You can bring me the money, and
take the hat back to him."

"And how much is your bill?" Presto asked.

"A hundred and thirty dollars."

Presto gasped. "Why he—he hasn't that much
money!"

"Oh, yes he has. He got it out of me tonight

with that fake offer you and he cooked up. Yes," said Freddy, "I think that's fair. Everybody will be satisfied. I'll have my profits from the show, and Zingo will have his hat at no cost to himself."

"But he has to have that money to live on," said the rabbit. "It's all he has."

"Where's all the money he got from the circus then?"

"Oh," said Presto, "he had to give that back."

This reply puzzled Freddy. He realized that they must be talking about two different things. The money he had referred to was the salary that Mr. Boomschmidt had paid Zingo for his work as a magician. But you don't "give back" your salary. Freddy thought quickly for a moment, then he shot a quick series of questions at the rabbit.

"Did he give back all of the money?"

"He lost a lot of it. He gave the rest back."

"Didn't he spend any of it at all?"

"He didn't have time."

"How much was there?"

"I think about a thousand dollars. But he hadn't counted it yet. Mr. Boo—" The rabbit stopped abruptly. "How do you know about this?" he demanded.

But Freddy had been rapidly putting two and two together. Zingo had got nearly a thousand dollars from the circus. It wasn't his salary. He had lost some of it and had had to give the rest back before spending, or even counting it. And since he had got it from the circus, he must have given it back to the circus—that is, Mr. Boomschmidt. Freddy said: "I know a great deal more than you think I do. I had a little talk with Mr. Boomschmidt before the circus left." Which was true enough, but of course nothing had been said about money.

Presto said angrily: "Mr. Boomschmidt had no right to tell you about it. He promised Signor Zingo that he would say nothing about it if he returned the part he had left and promised to pay the rest back when he got a job. He didn't want any scandal."

Freddy had the whole picture now. Zingo had evidently stolen money from the circus cashbox —probably during the confusion following the hurricane. Mr. Boomschmidt had found out, and in return for the five hundred or so that Zingo still had, had promised to say nothing about it. But he had fired Zingo from the show.

"Well," said Freddy, "I guess you'd better go back to Signor Zingo. You can tell him he can

have his hat if he sends me the money he took
out of the show tonight. But hold on a minute!" For Freddy had suddenly remembered the
scheme he had thought out for keeping Minx
quiet during the week of her stay. In order to
carry it out, he had to get Presto to show the
cat his disappearing trick.

"Look here," he said, "it's too late to do any
more tonight. But I'm going to hold you for
further questioning. Jinx, I wonder if you and
Minx would be willing to take this animal to
the bank, and stand guard over him till morning? It's the only place I can think of where he
can't escape."

The cats weren't very enthusiastic about this.
They would be comfortable enough, for the
Beans had contributed a couple of old
cushioned armchairs to the bank—the customers' chairs, Freddy called them, though he
always sat in the most comfortable one himself.
But one of them at least would have to stay
awake to keep an eye on Presto. Freddy per-
suaded them however by telling them about Signor Zingo's hat, and making the rabbit promise to show them his disappearing trick. Then,
satisfied that his plan was well under way, he said
goodnight to the others and trotted off home.

## Chapter 10

Freddy had an alarm clock that always went off an hour earlier than it was set for. He said he liked it better that way. If he had to get up at six, he set it for seven, and then although he really knew that he would be getting up at six, he could think as he dropped off to sleep: "Seven. I don't have to get up till seven." It didn't seem nearly as early doing it that way.

He set the clock for six the next morning,

and at five ten he was up and out—for it doesn't take a pig long to get dressed—and started to make a number of early morning calls. He called on Hank, and the cows, and Mr. Pomeroy, and Charles, and they all giggled and agreed to do what he wanted them to; and then he sent word to all the other animals on the farm. And after that was all settled he went down to the bank.

He opened the door and looked in. Jinx was curled up in one chair and Minx in the other, and Signor Zingo's hat was in the middle of the floor. The two rabbits who were the regular night guards were at their posts on the trap-door to the vaults. But there was no sign of Presto.

"Hey!" said Freddy. "Fine pair of jailers you are! Where's the prisoner? Escaped, I suppose?"

The cats jumped up and both began explaining at once. Presto had vanished. He had done his disappearing act in the hat for them several times, but the last time he had refused to reappear again. "Goodbye," he had said; "I'm going back to Centerboro," and after that hadn't answered when they spoke to him. "We thought he must still be in the room," Minx said, "because even though he was invisible, he would have to open the door to get out." But they had searched the place so thoroughly, even pawing about gingerly inside the hat, that they were sure they'd have caught him if he'd been there. He was just simply gone.

Freddy smiled to himself. He had a pretty good idea what had happened. Presto had probably got sick of hearing Minx talk, and had curled up quietly in the secret compartment of the hat. And indeed, when he spread a piece of paper over the hat and said: "Presto, change-o!" and took the paper off, there was the rabbit, sitting up and blinking sleepily at them.

Freddy went and opened the door. "All right, Presto," he said. "Beat it!" And in three jumps Presto was out of the hat, out of the door, and in the middle of the road. And he disappeared down the highway like a small white stone being skipped across water.

"What did you let him go for?" said Jinx. "We might have made him show us how to disappear too."

"Did I ever tell you about that conjuror I knew in India?" Minx asked. "He—"

"Sure, sure; forty times," Freddy cut in. "Listen, anybody can disappear in that hat. I'd like to do it myself, only I'm too big to get in it. But why don't one of you try it? How about you, Jinx?" He looked warningly at his friend and shook his head slightly, and Jinx, realizing that something was up, said: "Why, I'd like to, but—er—"

"Ladies first, eh?" said Freddy. "All right, Minx. You try."

So Minx got in and Freddy put the paper over her. He rattled it a good deal, and under cover of the sound whispered rapidly in Jinx's ear. Jinx's face broke into a delighted smile, and he stood back, and then Freddy said the magic words and whisked the paper off. And there of course was Minx, sitting in the hat.

"Just as I thought," said Freddy. "She's vanished all right."

"Completely gone," Jinx agreed.

"I'm right here," said Minx. "Do you really mean you can't see me?"

"Did you hear anything?" said Freddy.

"Thought I heard a faint mew," said Jinx. "Are you there, sis?" Both animals peered earnestly at a point just above Minx's head.

"Certainly I'm here," she said crossly. "Can't you even hear what I say?" She jumped out of the hat and walked over to Jinx and cuffed his ear.

Jinx didn't look at her. "Funny," he said; "I thought something just touched my ear. Very light and delicate, though—like a butterfly's kiss. Or I could have imagined it, I suppose."

"Probably," said Freddy, who was still peering into the hat, and feeling around the inside. "No, she's not here. Queer we don't hear her say anything, though. I could always hear Presto."

"You big ninnies!" said Minx angrily. "I'm right here in front of your stupid noses! Look at me, can't you?" And as they continued to gaze worriedly around into the corners of the room: "I don't like this!" she wailed. "You let me out of here!"

Freddy had gone over and was feeling of the chair cushions. "Not here," he said. "My goodness, Jinx, suppose she's really vanished. I mean, not just invisible, but really—gone! Wouldn't that be awful!"

"Terrible," said Jinx calmly.

"Your only sister, too," said Freddy.

"Yeah," said Jinx.

"I tell you what," Freddy said. "Let's try the

magic words again. Maybe she'll come back."
And as he picked up the paper, Minx jumped
back into the hat.

But the magic words didn't work. When
Freddy took off the paper, both he and Jinx
professed to be unable to see her. And though
she wailed and cried and protested and finally
called them a lot of unladylike names, they still
pretended she wasn't there. At last Freddy said:
"Well, there's no sense staying here. We can
come back later and try again."

"O K," said Jinx. "I expect she'll come back
some time—she always does. Of course, she's
really a darned nuisance with all that everlasting
gabble of hers, but I'd sort of hate to lose her
entirely, at that."

"Sure you would," said Freddy. "Sure you
would. After all, a sister's a sister, no matter how
silly."

"Ain't it the truth," said Jinx.

Minx followed them up to the barnyard. She
had stopped yelling by this time, because there's
not much satisfaction in bawling people out if
they don't hear you. I guess she had thought at
first that Freddy and Jinx were just putting up
a game on her. But when she reached the barnyard she was really convinced that she was in-

*"Well, there is no sense staying here."*

visible. For on his early calls that morning
Freddy had warned all the other animals to pretend that they couldn't see or hear her, and so
when the three of them walked into the cow
barn, the cows said good morning to Freddy and
Jinx and then asked where Minx was.

"Vanished," said Freddy sadly. "Disappeared. Dissipated into nothingness like the
smoke from yesterday's kitchen fire." And he
told them about it.

"Tut, tut," said the cows together; "how
dreadful!"

"Very sad," said Freddy. "Can't even have a
funeral, you see."

All the while Minx was walking up and down
in front of them, lashing her tail angrily, and
saying: "But I'm right here! Oh, darn you,
Freddy! I wish I'd never come to this horrible
farm!"

"Very sad for you, Jinx," said Mrs. Wiggins
soberly. "But we must look on the bright side
of things. Minx was a charming person, but if
you were with her very long you had to wear
ear plugs."

"Blessings sometimes come in disguise," said
Mrs. Wogus piously.

"Of course," said Mrs. Wurzburger, "if

there's anything we can do, don't hesitate to call on us."

"Thank you, my friends; thank you," said Jinx in a subdued voice. "You are all very kind. I suppose it will take some time for me to get used to the fact that Minx is no longer with me. Not to hear her voice going on, and on, and on . . ." He put a paw over his eyes.

The cows drooped their heads mournfully. Minx, with her tail sticking straight up in the air, walked past them, and the tip of her tail just brushed across their noses and tickled them. If she hadn't been so scared and mad, she would probably have thought of some better way of bothering them, for of course they all exploded at once in a tremendous sneeze, and Minx was blown right out of the barn door.

Freddy and Jinx exploded too, in a laugh. They straightened out their faces, and Freddy said: "Pardon my unseemly merriment. Unforgiveable at a time like this."

"Not at all, not at all," said Jinx. "I'm sure Minx would want us to be gay."

"I don't know what got into us," said Mrs. Wogus. "Touch of hay fever, perhaps."

"Your sister is not to be sneezed at," said Mrs. Wiggins.

All the rest of the day Minx had a pretty hard time. Wherever she went, the animals ignored her completely. She would try to break into a conversation with some bragging remark about something she had seen or done, just as she used to do, but the animals went right on talking without looking at her or giving any sign that they knew she was there. To Minx the queerest thing about it was that they were so often talking about her. That wouldn't have surprised her so much if they had been praising her, for of course she thought that she was pretty wonderful. But the things they were saying weren't nice at all. The first few times she heard someone say that she was a pest, and that it was a fine thing for everybody that she had vanished, she was angry and said to herself: "Pooh, they're just jealous of my superior brains!" But after a while it began to sink in that she wasn't nearly as popular as she had thought. And along in the afternoon she went back to the bank and curled up in a chair and tried unhappily to take a nap.

Freddy and Jinx, in the meantime, had hitched up Hank and driven down to Centerboro to get the sawing-in-two box and other magic paraphernalia. On the announcement board in front of the movie theatre was a big sign:

## SIGNOR ZINGO

Formerly with Boomschmidt's Stupendous
and Unexcelled Circus
Offers an evening of

## REAL MAGIC

Conjuring, Mind-reading, Illusions
Recently on this stage an amateur performed certain simple, rather childish tricks. Now come see a professional performance.

**Tuesday, Sept. 2**                    **8 P.M.**

*Admission 50¢*

## CHALLENGE

To any person or animal who can duplicate, or explain, any feat which I perform, I will give $10 in cash for each trick so exposed.

(signed) *ZINGO*

The three animals read it in silence. Then they looked at one another.

"My good grief!" said Hank. "Why, that's kind of an insult, ain't it, Freddy? Amateur—ain't that a fighting word?"

"Well, not really," Freddy said. "It's true.

But he's not a very good sport, calling my tricks childish."

"The big yap!" Jinx snarled.

"He's trying to make himself look like a good sport with that ten-dollar offer," said Freddy. "But he knows I can't duplicate his tricks. And though I can sort of guess how some of them are done, I can't really explain them. We know the sawing-in-two trick, but of course he won't take a chance doing that one."

"I'd like to give him a piece of my mind," said Hank. "With a couple of good hard iron horseshoes on the side."

"He isn't going to get away with it," Jinx said. "We'll—we'll . . . what'll we do, Freddy?"

Freddy shook his head. "I don't know. I don't think there's anything we can do. We can't explain or . . . Hey, wait a minute!" he said. "I bet I know! Look, are you two boys with me? I mean, it'll be burglary, sort of, and maybe trouble if we get caught, but—"

"Burglary?" said Jinx. "Boy, I've always wanted to burgle. Runs in the blood; my father went into burgling when he lost his voice and had to give up singing. He could go up the side of a house like he was walking up Main Street, and he could ooze through a crack you'd swear wouldn't accommodate a garter snake. But he oozed once too often. Lost half his tail when Mrs. McLanihan's icebox door blew shut just as he was starting home with a couple pounds round steak. Couldn't keep his balance on fences and roofs after that with only half a tail."

"OK, OK," said Freddy impatiently. "Your reminiscences of happy family life are delightful, but we've got a lot of work to do. How about you, horse? I don't mean we're going to steal anything. Just look over Zingo's magic equipment."

"Oh, sure," said Hank. "Anything you say, Freddy—burglary or what not. As long as it ain't murder. I kind of feel we ought to draw the line at murder."

"Oh, that's all right," said Freddy with a grin. "You've got to draw it somewhere, Hank. Well, come on; let's get that stuff. I want to go see the sheriff before we start home."

## Chapter 11

Minx, in the meantime, had been doing a lot of thinking. Usually she didn't think much; she didn't have time because she talked so incessantly. It would be a good thing for a lot of people to be invisible for a little while. It had certainly been a good thing for Minx. For she found that the idea her friends on the farm had of her wasn't at all the idea she thought they had. At first she didn't believe it. But when you have heard fifteen or twenty animals all express the opinion that you are a bore and a stuck-up know-it-all and a general nuisance that ought to be pushed over a nice quiet cliff somewhere —well, you begin to wonder if perhaps it isn't so.

All this was good for Minx. But some of the other thinking she did wasn't good for her at all. For she began to think of all the advantages there were in being invisible. And there were quite a lot. She got up after a while and went back to the barnyard to make use of them.

She went over to the farmhouse and sat down on the back porch. Inside was a clatter of dishes where Mrs. Bean was setting the table. Also there were smells inside—smells of roast chicken and of gravy; and little wisps of these delicious smells seeped out through the keyhole and went right up Minx's nose. She licked her chops. She was awfully hungry. Then she looked down at the generous saucer of milk Mrs. Bean had put out for her and made a face at it. Milk—pooh! Milk was for visible cats; invisible cats ate finer food. She sat still and waited.

Pretty soon Mr. Bean came stumping in from the barn and went in the back door, and Minx went in with him. The cats were in and out all day, so Mr. Bean never noticed her but went to the sink to scrub up for dinner. Minx ran into the dining room and jumped up on the table. The roast chicken was on a platter in front of Mr. Bean's place, and beside it was a bowl of gravy. The gravy was too hot to eat, but the chicken . . . Minx licked it delicately. Just pleasantly warm. She went to work on a drumstick.

And at that moment Mrs. Bean came in.

Minx never knew exactly what happened then. It must have been a good deal like Charles' experience in the hurricane. She had later a vague recollection of having been seized by the scruff of the neck, thrown to the floor, and then chased around the dining room, into the kitchen, under the stove, up the back stairs, down the front stairs . . . and then she was out in the barnyard, running for her life. It wasn't until, aching in every muscle as much from the unaccustomed exercise as from the whacks of the broom, she was back in the chair at the bank, that it occurred to her that Mrs. Bean had seen her.

"Why, I don't believe I'm invisible at all!" she said. She left the bank and went up along the road to the gate. Nobody was in sight in the barnyard. She crept cautiously up to the cow barn door and listened. And she heard Mrs.

Wogus say: "Well, a joke's a joke, but if you carry it too far it gets to be something else. And if we drive that poor cat crazy pretending she's invisible—"

Georgie's voice interrupted. "She's crazy now, if you ask me," he said. "Anybody's crazy that tells such awful lies. Remember that story about how she went hunting in India and killed an elephant?"

"Maybe she talked him to death," said Henrietta's voice.

Minx didn't listen to any more. She went back to the bank to plan her revenge. "You just wait, my fat friend!" she thought. "And you too, my darling little brother! You cooked this up between you. Well, wait till you get a taste of *my* cooking!"

Freddy and Jinx, in the meantime, had gone to call on the sheriff. They found him in his little office in the jail, deep in conversation with Mr. Ollie Groper, proprietor of the Centerboro Hotel.

"We'll come back later if you're busy," said Freddy, but the sheriff said: "No, no; come in. Maybe you can help us. Ollie's got some trouble on his hands and we've been discussin' it for an hour, but for all the good it's done, we might as well have been hollerin' down a well."

"The problem," said Mr. Groper in a deep bass voice, "appears like it's insoluble." He was a large fat man with a large bald head and he sat in the sheriff's armchair as if it had been built around him. He looked, Jinx said afterwards, as if he was all crated up and ready to ship.

"Well, let's hear what Freddy's got on his mind," said the sheriff. "My guess is it's got something to do with Zingo, and if so, we'll all put our heads together and if we can't work out some plan of action, why brains ain't what they were when I was a boy." He winked at Freddy. "Kind of upset about this show he's giving, are you?"

"Why yes, we are," Freddy said. "He and that Presto pulled a fast one on me last night."

"Got into him for a hundred and thirty smackers," put in Jinx.

"And I want to get back at him," Freddy continued. "So I thought, you being in town, you could maybe let me know when he moves all his magic apparatus over into the theatre, and then we could come down and . . . well, I've got a plan."

"I bet you have," said the sheriff enthusiastically. "I bet you have!" He turned to Mr. Groper. "If you want to get rid of Zingo, Ollie, my advice to you is to hire Frederick (which is this pig) and Wiggins (which is a cow that ain't here at the moment) to do the job for you. For it's a detective job, and they're far and away the best detectives in the county. O' course, far as I know there ain't any other detectives *in* the county, but I don't take back a word of what I just said."

Mr. Groper nodded his big head slowly. "I been apprised previous of their investigating faculties," he said. "Proclivities which I can truly say ain't usually inherent in the bovine or porcine races."

"Wow!" said Freddy, and caught himself up quickly. "I mean, yes sir, I guess that's so. But you—you're having trouble with Zingo, Mr. Groper? He's staying at your hotel, isn't he?"

"A temporary resident of that caravansary," Mr. Groper replied, "which I would gladly expedite his departure to a higher sphere with a club, only it ain't feasible."

"You mean you want to get rid of him?" Freddy asked. "Why don't you throw him out?"

"Mister," said the hotelkeeper, "when a guest discovers cyprinodontidae in the milk pitcher and conjures arachnids and larvae of some of them lepidoptera onto the edge of the salad bowl, you let him do what he pleases."

"Yeah," said Freddy weakly, "I guess you do."

The sheriff laughed. "Guess I'd better tell you," he said. "Ollie here got a dictionary by the tail when he was in school and he ain't never let go. Why, this is the trouble. Zingo went to stay at the hotel, and everything was smooth as butter until the end of the first week Ollie give him his bill. Zingo sticks it in his pocket and goes in to dinner. Pretty soon out comes the waitress with a pitcher of milk, and she shows Ollie how there's a minnow swimmin' around in it."

"Cyprinoid," put in Mr. Groper.

"And then," continued the sheriff, "out comes Zingo and hands Ollie the bill and he says: 'Just receipt this for me, Mr. Groper.'

" 'Yeah?' says Ollie. 'Why?' Or some good long words to that effect.

" 'Because,' says Zingo, 'if 'twas to get around that folks found things like that in the food, there ain't anybody that would stay at this hotel.' 'Well, Ollie knew Zingo had put the minnow in the milk himself, all right, but he couldn't prove it, and if it was get out it would be awful bad for business. So he receipted the bill. But that night he give Zingo notice to leave.

"And the next morning Zingo finds a live treetoad in his orange juice, and he goes to Ollie and says he's going to sue the hotel.

"Well, what can Ollie do? He has to let him stay. And every time he says anything about the bill, Zingo pulls some such stunt. Last night there was a traveling man named Giblet or some such name having his supper in the dining room, and Zingo stops at his table and says excuse me and picks a couple of them fuzzy caterpillars off the edge of his plate, and Giblet jumps up and grabs his bag and beats it.

"OK, you got any ideas?"

"Why, good gracious," said Freddy, "no, not at the moment. But let's see—today's Thursday —there's five days before Zingo's show. Now if I could stay at the hotel as a guest those five days . . . How about it, Mr. Groper? It would give me a chance to make my own preparations for Zingo's show, and I'm pretty certain we could find some way of getting rid of him for you."

"The benefits of such a plan seem highly problematical," said Mr. Groper. "Your features being recognizably porcine, and this necromancer bein' a perspicacious individual and fully cognizant of same, I'd say we'd become involved in unpredictable eventualities terminating in a highly detrimental denouement, catastrophic in its scope."

"You took the words right out of my mouth," said Jinx with a grin.

But Freddy said: "I guess you mean he'd recognize me. But I'd be in disguise of course."

Mr. Groper fired a string of polysyllables which Freddy took to mean that he didn't think any disguise would work, but the sheriff reassured him. Freddy, he said, was a master of disguise. "You remember that time," he said to Freddy, "when you wore that old-fashioned sailor suit that used to belong to Mr. Bean, and you stayed here for weeks and nobody knew you? Why, I believe that suit's still here. You could be Ollie's nephew, come for a visit." He glanced from the pig to Mr. Groper and back again; there certainly was a sort of family resemblance between them, though he didn't say so. "Wait; I'll get it."

Freddy was a little thinner that summer than he had been on the previous occasion when he had worn the suit. They didn't have to tug so hard to get him into it. And Mr. Groper was

*And the next morning Zingo finds a live treetoad in his orange juice.*

much impressed. There was even, he said, a distinct resemblance to his brother Mervyn's boy, Marshall.

"Fine," said the sheriff. "You'll give out that Marshall has come to visit you. You better go right over to the hotel now and get settled."

But Freddy said he wouldn't be able to until later in the day. There were a number of arrangements to be made at the farm, and of course he would have to get Mr. Bean's permission. So they shook hands all around, and then Freddy and Jinx left.

They were too busy when they got home to make much of a search for Minx, who had apparently really disappeared during their absence. Nobody had seen her for some time. But there was nothing to worry about. She could take care of herself, and she would find out soon enough that she wasn't really invisible. So they put Zingo's hat back in the bank vault, guarded by the two rabbits, and went ahead with their plans and interviews. And late in the afternoon they hitched up Hank and drove down to Centerboro again.

## Chapter 12

Disguised as Marshall Groper, Freddy walked into the hotel lobby. He hadn't worn the sailor suit after all. For one thing, it was fifty years behind the style, and for another, Freddy felt that he looked foolish in it. Which of course he did. So he went into the Busy Bee Department Store and bought an Indian suit, complete with feathered war bonnet and fringed leggings and maybe he looked foolish in that too, but the war bonnet was certainly a good idea, for it partially concealed the feature that was most likely to give him away—his long nose.

Nobody paid any attention to the rather stout little boy in the Indian suit who put his suitcase down by the desk and was warmly greeted by Mr. Groper. He was shown up to a room which Mr. Groper said was "contiguous to that currently occupied by Signor Zingo." Freddy had brought a small dictionary along, for he thought it might be useful in his conversations with his new uncle, and he got it out of the suitcase and found what contiguous meant.

Then he unpacked the suitcase and I guess a lot of people would have been surprised to see what was in it. There were four mice in it, for one thing, and they were pretty cross, for they had been shaken up quite a lot when the porter had carried the bag upstairs. Jinx was in it, too, and there were some tools (for burgling operations), and a couple of spare disguises, and a notebook and pencil (in case Freddy felt like poetry), and some magic apparatus, and a toothbrush, and a lot of other things. And the last thing Freddy took out was a small box in which were his friends, Mr. and Mrs. Webb, the spiders. Freddy let them out right away, and they went for a walk on the ceiling to stretch their legs.

As soon as he had got things unpacked and put neatly away in bureau drawers, Freddy gave his friends their instructions. He could hear Signor Zingo moving around in the next room, so he was careful to speak very low. There was a locked door between the two rooms, and he set the mice to work gnawing a hole in the lower corner. Then after the Webbs were rested, he had them try the keyhole. But the key was in it on the other side and they couldn't get through.

"Maybe his window's open," said Mr. Webb. "If you'll put up this window I'll walk across and see." So Freddy opened the window, and in a few minutes Mr. Webb came back. Freddy put his ear down close to the spider. "Shut," said Mr. Webb. "But he's there. Practicing card tricks in front of the mirror. And Presto's asleep on the bed."

"OK," said Freddy. "Boys," he said to the mice, "you're making an awful racket with that gnawing. Maybe you'd better lay off until Zingo goes down to supper."

The mice stopped working. "Freddy thinks we're too gnawsy," said Eek, and they all laughed uproariously. Though of course there wasn't much uproar—only squeaks.

Freddy went down early to supper. He wanted to get into the dining room before Zingo did. He sat with Mr. Groper at a table in a corner with his back to the rest of the room. But the magician, when he came in, walked straight over to their table.

"Ah, Mr. Groper," he said, "I see you have company. Present me to your little guest."

Mr. Groper said: "Signor Zingo—Marshall Groper, consanguineous with me on the paternal side, him being offspring of my fraternal relative."

"Well, that's one way of looking at it," said the magician, and held out his hand. "How do you do, Marshall?"

"I do all ride, thag you," said Freddy in a stuffed-up voice, and sniffed. He pretended to have a cold to disguise his voice. He didn't shake hands, and Zingo drew his hand back and put it in his pocket.

"You don't seem very glad to see me," he said. "I guess you don't know who I am, do you, Marshall?"

"Sure," said Freddy; "I doe who you are, you're the bagiciad that do'd ever pay by uggle adythig."

Zingo pretended that he hadn't understood.

"I don't ever what? Has the boy got an impediment in his speech?" he asked Mr. Groper.

Mr. Groper started to say something, but Freddy said: "I guess you've got an impediment in your pocketbook, haven't you?" Only of course all his m's were b's, and all his n's were d's. When you read it you can hold your nose and it will sound the way it did when Freddy said it.

"Dear me," said Zingo, "what a rude little boy!" He stared distastefully at Freddy who was trying to keep his face turned away. "And why, Mr. Groper, do you let him come to the table with a false face on?"

"Gee, I wonder if he has recognized me!" Freddy thought. "I guess I'd better get rid of him." He said in a loud voice: "I should think you'd be ashamed to come in this dining room, when you don't ever pay your hotel bill!"

Everybody in the dining room stared, and Mr. Groper said: "Ain't you being a little contumelious, Marshall?"

Signor Zingo smiled his tight smile and put a hand on Freddy's shoulder. "Oh, come, my little man," he said, and pinched the shoulder viciously.

Freddy gave a loud squeal and wriggled away.

"He pinched me!" he squalled. "The big bully!" And he began to cry.

Signor Zingo took his hand away quickly. He looked around at the other diners with raised eyebrows. Everyone glared, and a voice said: "Shame!"

"Aw, I never touched the big baby!" said Zingo; then he shrugged and went on to his table, where he sat with his back to Freddy, fingering his moustache.

Freddy felt that he had made a good beginning. Zingo's temper had betrayed him, and the story of how he had maltreated a child would go all over town, for a number of Centerboro business men had witnessed the performance. As a disguise, the Indian suit had been a good idea. And the war bonnet was the best part of it, for it was built up with a circle of eagle feathers around the head and a long tail of eagle feathers down the back, and so when people looked at it they just looked at the headdress and not so much at the face under it. That was probably the reason why nobody recognized Freddy, or saw that the face under the war bonnet was a pig's and not a little boy's.

After dinner Freddy went up to his room. The

mice had gnawed through the door, and had gone into Zingo's room, but they hadn't been able to look around much because Presto was still there. The Webbs, however, had gone in, and had spun themselves a little hammock up in a corner of the ceiling where they could sit comfortably and see and hear everything that went on. For the moment there wasn't anything to be done, so Freddy took off his war bonnet, got out his pencil and paper, and settled down to a little poetry.

This is what he wrote:

*O the swallows fly about the sky,*
   *And they swoop among the trees,*
*And they catch small bugs in their little mugs*
   *And swallow them down with ease.*

   *It's fun, no doubt, to whirl about*
      *In a swift and airy jig;*
   *But as for me, I'd much rather be*
      *A pig.*

*The rabbit, at night, when the moon is bright,*
   *Waits till it's nearly dawn;*
*Then out he hops, with his friends plays cops*
   *And robbers upon the lawn.*

*It's fun, I suppose, to wriggle your nose*
*And live on a lettuce diet;*
*But it's not my dish, and I wouldn't wish*
*To try it.*

*O cats are slim and full of vim*
*And they stay out late at night;*
*They're merry blades, who sing serenades*
*On the fence, by the moon's pale light.*

*It may be fun to wash with your tongue*
*And sing like the late Caruso,*
*But I'll tell you square, I wouldn't care*
*To do so.*

*Now take the pig. His brains aren't much big-*
*ger than cats' or swallows' or rabbits',*
*But in debate his words carry weight,*
*And he's formed very regular habits.*

*Pigs know all the answers; they're conceded as*
*dancers,*
*To be light as a bird on a twig.*
*So it mustn't gall you if people call you*
*A pig.*

He was polishing up the last two stanzas, which seemed to have too many words in them, though he heartily concurred in the sentiments expressed, when Mr. Webb crawled up over the edge of the paper and began waving his feelers to attract his attention.

"News for you, Freddy," said the spider. "Minx has just called on Zingo. She's told him that his hat was in the bank—our bank, I mean —and he's getting ready to go out there and break into the bank and get it."

"Wow!" said Freddy, jumping up, and the poem fell unnoticed to the floor. It was later picked up by the chambermaid, who was so impressed by the lazy happy life led by pigs that she cried for several days because she couldn't be one.

Jinx and the mice, who had been asleep on the bed, jumped up too, and they crowded around Mr. Webb to hear his story. Minx had wanted to get back at Freddy for the trick he had played on her, so she had told Signor Zingo that his magic hat was in the First Animal Bank.

"But I know that," Zingo had said. "Presto saw it there."

"But you don't know how to get it," Minx said.

No, the magician had said; he didn't. He understood the place was guarded night and day. And he wasn't going to give Freddy any hundred and thirty dollars for its return.

So Minx said she knew how to get in, and if he'd take her out there she'd help him get it.

"Well, come on," said Freddy. "What are we waiting for?"

"You can't beat them to it," said Mr. Webb. "He's getting ready to leave now, in his car."

"Then so are we," Freddy said. "Come on, Jinx. You others stay here."

"Watch out for Zingo," said Mr. Webb. "He's got a pistol."

They hustled down the back stairs and into the garage, and when a few minutes later Minx and Zingo came out and got into the car, the two animals were already in it, huddled together under a rug in the back seat.

As soon as they were out of town Zingo stepped on the accelerator and the car bounded swiftly up the road to the Bean farm. And Freddy and Jinx bounded with it. Freddy had thought that he could think up a plan of action on the way out, but he was too busy hanging on, and keeping from being smothered under the rug and being clawed by Jinx, to do much connected thinking. Jinx of course couldn't see anything, and to keep from being thrown about and bruised, he dug his claws into whatever was handy, and as Freddy was a good deal handier than anything else he dug them into Freddy. Freddy said afterwards that if he could have squealed it would have been much easier.

Zingo drove beyond the Bean farm, turned around, and then drove back and stopped the car a little beyond the bank. He and Minx got out and Minx said: "If you cut that bell rope high up, next to the clapper, then if the guards get away from us they can't reach it to ring the alarm." And before Freddy and Jinx got disentangled and out of the car, they heard Zingo open the bank door.

"Darn it!" said Jinx disgustedly. "Are we stuck or are we stuck?"

"Yeah," said Freddy. "We can't capture him now. But wait! Help me get this rug out and up to where they climbed the fence."

There was commotion in the bank and a flashlight flickered through the window as they dragged the rug up to the rail fence. Freddy whispered his instructions, and then they waited. Pretty soon the beam of the flashlight shot down towards them and was then shut off, and they heard Zingo's footsteps. He climbed the fence cautiously and behind him a little black shadow leaped to the top rail. But as it jumped down, Freddy, with the rug spread out, fell upon it. There was a great scrabbling and thrashing as Freddy struggled to pin Minx down and wind her in the rug.

"What's the matter?" Zingo whispered. "Don't make so much noise!" He stopped and directed the flashlight back at the sound, but Jinx stepped forward into the light.

"Nothing," he said. "Put out that light! I just bumped my nose in the dark."

Of course all cats look alike at night, and even in the daytime it wasn't easy to tell Jinx and Minx apart. Jinx was all black, while Minx had a white chest and white forepaws. But Zingo didn't notice the difference. "Well, come along," he said.

By the time they reached the car, Freddy had Minx well wound up in the rug, and her squalls were so muffled that nobody could hear them a few feet away. He tucked her under one arm, climbed the fence, and hid behind the bank.

Just as Zingo, with his magic hat on his head, was getting into the car, Jinx said: "Say, look! while we're here, why don't we take all the money that's in the bank vaults?"

"What money?" said Zingo.

"Why, Freddy keeps all his money there—and he made a lot last year with the circus. Mr. Bean has some money deposited there, too. And all the other animals. I bet there's more than a thousand dollars."

"Go on!" said Zingo incredulously. "You mean all that money is in an unprotected hole in the ground under that trapdoor? You're kidding me."

"But I'm not," said Jinx. "Oh well, go on if you want to. I'm not going to let this chance go," and he started back.

Zingo hesitated a moment, then he followed. As soon as they were in the bank, Freddy crept around to the door. Zingo lifted the trap, and the rabbits, whom he had shoved down into the vaults on his previous visit, and who had been ineffectually banging on the under side of the floor in the hope that someone would hear them, skittered off down the underground passage.

"Better let me get it," said Jinx. "That passage is a tight squeeze for you, and it goes quite a way before you get to the room where the money is."

"No doubt," said Zingo suspiciously. "But I prefer to go myself. Just in case," he said with his thin smile, "there's another way out. You might get mixed up and go out the other end with the money."

Jinx knew that there wasn't any other way out, but he tried to look disconcerted, as if he had really intended to sneak off with the money. So he held up the trapdoor and Zingo crawled down the passage. And as soon as the magician's feet had disappeared, he slammed down the door with a bang, and Freddy rushed in and they piled all the furniture in the bank on top of it. And Freddy added his weight by sitting down in one of the chairs, while Jinx rushed out to climb the tree from which the bell hung, to give the alarm.

The passage to the vaults was just about big enough to let Zingo crawl along on all fours, holding the flashlight ahead of him. When he heard the bang, he knew that he had been trapped, and he tried to turn around. But he couldn't. He had to go on until he came to the first room. So that by the time he got back to the trapdoor, the big bell was sending its clang-dong-bang! out over the dark and silent fields of the Bean farm.

Up in the cow barn Mrs. Wiggins heard it. "Trouble at the bank!" she shouted. "Come on, girls!" And followed by her two sisters she dashed out into the barnyard. As they galloped down across the fields towards the bank Robert and Georgie went bounding past them, while behind them they heard the clatter and thump of Hank's iron shoes as he backed out of his stall and followed.

On her perch in the henhouse Henrietta heard it. She popped her head out from under her wing, and pecked Charles sharply on the shoulder. "Trouble at the bank! Stop that snoring and wake up!"

"Wh-what's that?" Charles squawked. "Who hit me? Oh, it's you, Henrietta. What's the idea? I was just dreaming that—"

"Well, you aren't dreaming now," she interrupted, "and that's the alarm bell."

"The bank!" shouted the rooster, who suddenly remembered the peck of shelled corn and the fifty cents in cash that he had put in the vault for safekeeping. "Henrietta, you stay with the children. You'll be quite safe if you lock the door. I must get down there right away!"

"Oh, yes?" said Henrietta sarcastically. "And what good would you be, may I ask? You'll stay with the children yourself!" And she fluttered down and out of the door.

Up on the edge of the woods Sniffy Wilson,

the skunk, heard it. He was out hunting with two of his boys. "Trouble at the bank!" he said. "Edgar, you run back and get your mother and the other children, and Thurlow, you run over and wake up Mr. Grundy, the woodchuck. He sleeps like a log—he'll never hear the bell."

And up in the Big Woods Old Whibley heard it. He had just swooped on a mouse but had miscalculated the distance and had come down rather heavily among some blackberry canes, while the mouse ran off giggling, and his niece, Vera, who was hunting with him, pretended not to have noticed. "Trouble at the bank!" he hooted. "Wretched animals—always in trouble! Always coming for help—most inconvenient times. Well, come along, Vera! Don't just sit there!" And he spread his wings and floated softly down towards the bank.

Most of the animals, as they galloped along through the dark, could see only well enough to avoid running into trees or falling over fences. By the thump and patter of hoofs and paws all about them they knew that other animals were running beside them, but they had no idea whether they were many or few. But the owls, who can see fairly well except on the very darkest nights, had the whole farm spread below them. They saw dozens and dozens of animals all converging headlong on the bank—cows and dogs; Hank, and Bill the goat, and goodness knows how many rabbits; and there were skunks and woodchucks lolloping along with their clumsy gait, and a fox or two; and they saw Peter, the bear, and his two cousins, break from the woods and streak down the hill at a dead run. And all around them in the night sky were chirps and the flutter and beat of wings, for the birds were coming too.

Up in the farmhouse Mr. Bean heard it in his sleep. He stirred uneasily and mumbled: "Dinner! Land sakes, dinner time already?" Then he woke up. "Mrs. B.! Mrs. B.!" he said. "That's the old dinner bell down on Freddy's bank!" He leaped out of bed, pulled on his boots, grabbed his shotgun, and in his long white nightshirt and his white nightcap with the red tassel, tumbled down the stairs and out into the darkness.

Down at the bank Freddy had lit a candle so he could see what was going on. He sat in the chair, trying to make himself as heavy as possible as the trapdoor under him shook with the heaves of the enraged magician. He still held Minx, who had stopped struggling inside the blanket.

The bell clanged and bonged and made so much noise that he couldn't hear whether his friends were coming to his rescue or not; but he didn't need to hear them—he knew they'd come.

Then the scrabbling down in the passage stopped, and after a moment's quiet there was a muffled bang, and something zipped up past Freddy and went through the roof with a click. For maybe half a second he looked up at the little round hole in the boards above his head. Then he gave a squeal and threw himself sideways so that he and the chair and Minx went over in a heap. And when presently the trap-door was forced slowly up, and Signor Zingo's sharp nose and a shiny pistol barrel appeared side by side in the crack, Freddy was outside peeking in.

Zingo crawled out. He was covered with dirt and the expression on his face wasn't pleasant to see. Outside, the bell had stopped ringing, and he could hear plainly the rush and trampling as the animals closed in. For a moment he hesitated; his magic hat had been knocked off in the passage and left there; but there was no time to go back for it. He ran out the door and made for the fence.

He was just in time. As he went over the

*Then he gave a squeal and threw himself sideways.*

fence, Robert made a snatch at him, but the collie's narrow jaws snapped shut on the tail of the long red-lined cape. Robert held on, and Zingo went on without it, just as Mrs. Wogus and Bill, the goat, came crashing into the fence behind him.

The fence held up the pursuit just long enough for Zingo to reach his car. The smaller animals went through or over, but alone they were too weak to tackle the magician, and the bears, who could have gotten over easily, hadn't yet come up. The two dogs got over, but the car door was shut and Zingo was inside stepping on the starter before they could reach him. And by the time Hank had turned around and kicked enough rails out of the fence so the animals could pour through, the car had begun to move.

Zingo had a terrible temper, and the thought of being done out of his hat and a thousand dollars by a lot of farm animals made him lose it completely. He glanced back and saw that the chase had been given up; the mob of animals made a darker blot on the darkness of the road behind him. He stopped the car with a jerk, leaned out, and aimed his pistol to shoot into the crowd. And Old Whibley, who had been cruising along, waiting for a chance, swept noiselessly down. His long sharp talons closed on Zingo's hand, and the magician gave a yell and dropped the pistol. Vera swooped and picked it up, and as Zingo, grinding his teeth with pain and anger, drove on towards Centerboro, the two owls, without saying anything to Freddy, flew back to their nest.

Back in the road everyone was shouting at once and asking questions, and Freddy was trying to explain, when they heard the clump, clump of Mr. Bean's boots coming along the road. The voices died down to a respectful silence as the farmer came up. It was like Mr. Bean not to ask any questions. He always said that if his animals needed his help, he was there to give it; otherwise he thought it was better for them to manage their own affairs.

All he said now was: "Everything all right?"

"Yes, sir," said Freddy. "It was a burglar. We drove him off."

Mr. Bean gave a grunt which might have meant anything. Freddy thought it meant: "Good work!" but it might just as well have meant: "Lot of fuss about nothing!" Then he said: "Pretty late. Better get to bed." And turned and stumped off.

But the animals weren't as easily satisfied.

Freddy had to explain everything, and make a little speech thanking them all. It was nearly eleven o'clock when he and Jinx at last started back for Centerboro with the red-lined cape in a bundle under his arm.

## Chapter 13

Freddy had dropped Minx when he had fallen
out of his chair in the bank and nothing had
been seen of her since. He and Jinx agreed that
probably nothing would be seen of her for some
time to come. The farm wouldn't be a very
pleasant place for her, and they both felt that
she had probably started out on her travels again
and that the next that would be heard of her
would be a postcard from Quebec or Buenos
Aires, with a line or two saying that she was be-

ing entertained by the mayor and had been given the keys of the city.

They were pretty surprised therefore when she overtook them a mile down the road.

At first they wouldn't have anything to do with her. She begged and pleaded to be allowed to come with them. "I don't know what got into me to do a thing like that, Freddy," she said. "I was mad at the trick you played on me, but really and truly I am terribly sorry, and I'll do anything if you will forgive me."

Freddy didn't say anything, but Jinx said: "You'd better stay invisible, sis, if you know what's good for you. I'm your brother or I'd knock your head off; but there are a lot of animals back there that aren't your brother, and you'd better keep away from them."

Minx said meekly that she wished he would knock her head off—she'd feel better about it; and she followed them, weeping and wailing, until Freddy finally took pity on her. "Look here, Minx," he said, "if you really mean it— well, I know you won't go to see Zingo, after tonight—he thinks you shut him in the bank vault. So if you want to come along with us, and will promise to do just as we tell you, and not talk us deaf, dumb and blind . . ."

"Oh, I will, Freddy," Minx said. "I mean I won't. I won't say a word, I promise; I'll be just as still—you won't hear a thing out of me, not a whisper—"

"And *now,*" Freddy interrupted firmly, "is the time to begin."

So Minx stopped talking and didn't say another word all the way to Centerboro.

When they got back to the hotel the mice told them that Zingo had come in about half an hour before and had gone right to bed. But during his absence they had ransacked the room. They had found a lot of gadgets he used in doing tricks, and they described these to Freddy, and in one of his pockets they had found a box containing a number of beetles and caterpillars.

"We let 'em out," said Quik. "Poor things, they were almost suffocated. I hope it was all right to do that, Freddy. We thought it was cruelty to animals or something."

"Cruelty to bugs," said Freddy, "which is just as bad, though lots of people don't think so. Sure it was all right. I suppose he's collected them to drop around on people's plates in the dining room if Mr. Groper starts talking about his bill again."

"They were awful grateful," said Eek. "They said if they could ever do anything to pay us back, just to call on them."

Some people would have laughed at the idea that the assistance of a caterpillar or a beetle could be of any value, but Freddy had had extensive contacts with the insect world, and their help had at times been invaluable to him. He said: "Where are they now?"

"We opened the window for them," said Quik, "but they said they guessed they'd stick around until you came back, just in case. They're there on the sill."

There were two large red-brown fuzzy caterpillars, and several smaller smooth green ones, and half a dozen assorted beetles, standing in a little group on the window sill. Freddy went over and thanked them for their offer, and then he called up Room Service and had some lettuce sent up for their supper. The fuzzy caterpillars didn't like lettuce, and the beetles never ate it, but they didn't like to say so when Freddy had gone to so much trouble, so they all politely ate a little. Then the caterpillars, who are not used to being out so late, curled up and went to sleep. I don't know what the beetles did; they are like some people—it is hard to tell whether they are

asleep or just thinking. But the green caterpillars liked lettuce and they sat up and ate it
all night. They were quite a lot larger in the
morning.

The mice also reported that several mouse-
traps had been set in dark corners of Zingo's
room. "He probably heard us gnawing yesterday," said Eeny, "Or maybe Presto saw us."

"You'd better be careful and not go fooling
around there in the dark," said Freddy.

Eeny grinned. "We put 'em where they'd do
the most good. I guess he hasn't hit the one we
put in his bed yet. But there's a couple others
will get him sooner or later."

"That gives me an idea," said Freddy. "Re-
mind me to buy a few tomorrow. And I think
we'd better get some sleep; we've got a lot to
do before Tuesday."

Freddy was having breakfast with Mr.
Groper next morning when Signor Zingo came
into the dining room. He came straight up to
their table, and Freddy was horrified to see that
he had the cape with the red lining over his arm.
The last Freddy had seen of it was when he had
thrown it over the back of a chair in his own
room when he had come in last night.

"Morning, Groper," said the magician.

"Maybe you can explain why I find this cape of mine in your nephew's bedroom, eh? What kind of a hotelkeeper are you anyway? Serving caterpillars with the meals, and now having a sneak thief come to stay with you! If you've got anything to say before I call the police—"

Everybody in the dining room had stopped eating and was staring, and two guests who had come the night before got up and left the room hurriedly—presumably to check up and see if any of their belongings were missing.

Freddy said quickly: "I found this cape last night and took it to my room. It was too late to find out who it belonged to. Go ahead and call the police. I guess they'll want to know how you got into my room—the door was locked."

"I had a right to go in after my own property," said Zingo. "I've suspected you were a crook all along, though it is hard to believe that one so young could be so depraved. But I suppose this uncle of yours put you up to it."

Mr. Groper heaved himself to his feet. "You state," he said, "that this here article of apparel is one of your chattels and appurtenances." He seized the cape and examined it. "Tain't provided with any legend, label or device that determines such ownership." He tossed the cape back. "But I'm with you as to the advisability of summoning the representatives of the law. This young relative of mine has had his constitutional rights violated and trompled on. His private room has been burglariously and feloniously broke into. And I'm agoing to put myself into immediate telephonic communication with the sheriff." He started for the office.

Zingo evidently realized that he had gone too far. He had found his cape in the room occupied by Mr. Groper's nephew—but how had he got into that room? He had no wish to explain that to a judge. So he merely grumbled something about living in a den of thieves, and sat down to his breakfast pulling his moustache irritably as he ordered an extra portion of ham and eggs.

Freddy was worried. If Zingo had broken into his room, he might have discovered a good deal. He might have discovered that little Marshall Groper was just a pig in an Indian suit. And a pig who was his enemy. Freddy would have liked to go upstairs at once and find out what had happened. But he didn't dare leave the dining room until the sheriff came. For although it would please Mr. Groper to have Zingo arrested and taken off to jail, it would mean that Freddy would probably never get his hundred and thirty dollars back. It would mean that there would be no magic show Tuesday night, and Freddy had laid very elaborate plans for that show. Also it would mean that the sheriff would have a very troublesome prisoner in his jail. For Zingo certainly wouldn't fit in well with the other prisoners, who, as the sheriff often said, were just one big happy family.

Presently Mr. Groper came back and sat down with the remark that the representative of legal authority was momentarily anticipated.

"You mean the sheriff's coming," said Freddy, who was getting used to Mr. Groper's language.

Mr. Groper smiled a slow, fat, kindly smile. "You—and—Sheriff," he said very slowly, as if choosing his words with great care, "are about —the only ones—that ever know what—I'm talking about. You see, I've always had a predilection for this here sesquipedalianism. I . . ."

"Whoa!" Freddy interrupted. "Now you're way beyond me."

Mr. Groper nodded. "I mean," he said, "big words. They were—kind of a hobby. Which it is bad. It habituates you to imperspicuity. I mean—you can't find the little words when you want 'em. So that I ain't able any longer to express myself in intelligible monosyllables. And though my oral communication is unambiguous, it . . ."

A loud yell and the scrape of a chair interrupted him. Freddy turned around. Zingo, who had put a hand in his pocket to get a cigar, had yanked it out again and jumped to his feet. From one finger dangled a mousetrap.

"Look at that!" he shouted furiously. "That's the kind of thing that goes on in this miserable dump you call a hotel!" He shook his fist at Mr. Groper who was slowly getting his feet under him so he could get out of his chair. "Treetoads in the orange juice, sneak thieves going through your rooms, and now practical jokes! And I know who's responsible! If you won't give this nasty little wretch a good hiding, I'll do it myself, and now!" And as he advanced upon Freddy he whipped off his belt and swung it menacingly.

Freddy slid out of his chair and ducked around behind Mr. Groper, who by now was halfway up. He didn't like the look of that belt buckle, and he knew the magician meant business. But just as Zingo reached for him, a voice from the doorway said: "What's going on here?" It was the sheriff.

One of the guests pointed at Zingo. "That fellow got caught in a mousetrap," he said. "He's going to lick the boy for putting it in his pocket."

"Caught in a mousetrap, eh?" said the sheriff. He shook his head. "Tryin' to steal the cheese, I suppose. What some folks won't do to get a little extra!"

"I wasn't stealing the cheese, you fool!" snarled Zingo. "That boy put the trap in my pocket."

"Kin you prove it?" said the sheriff. "And if so, what of it? Tain't a hangin' matter. Whereas this breakin' into the boy's room—"

"I don't think he broke into it," Freddy interrupted. "I remember now I left the door open, and if he saw his cape there, I suppose it was all right to go in and get it."

The sheriff and Mr. Groper stared at Freddy in puzzlement. Why, they wondered, was he throwing away a chance to have the magician locked up? Zingo was puzzled too. But he had the good sense to go back to his chair.

The sheriff turned to Mr. Groper. "Well, Ollie," he said, "I don't see as there is anything for me to do here. Unless," he said to Zingo,

*A loud yell and the scrape of a chair interrupted him.*

"you want to make charges against this wild Indian for illegally and with malice afore-thought settin' traps, gins, slings or snares with the intent of catchin' and pinchin' one or more digits, and thus causin' you pain, alarm and vexation of spirit? How's that, Ollie?" he said, grinning at the hotelkeeper.

But Mr. Groper was too disappointed at not being able to have Zingo arrested to applaud the sheriff's elegant language. He merely shrugged and lumbered off towards the office.

The magician didn't bother to reply either. He lit a cigar and called for another cup of coffee.

When the sheriff had gone, Freddy slipped up to his room.

"Hi, Big Chief Pretzel Tail," said Jinx. "Take off that war bonnet: we know you. Say, there's been a visitor to your wigwam while you were out."

"I know it," said Freddy. "How'd he get in?"

"With a key. We heard him try two or three, and then he got one that unlocked the door. Minx and I hid in the closet. I don't think he came in to get his cape, because he acted surprised when he saw it. And he looked in all the bureau drawers."

"He must suspect who I am," said Freddy. "If he thought I was just Mr. Groper's nephew, he wouldn't snoop in here, and if he knew who I was, I don't think he would either. He's looking for evidence."

"Well, he didn't get much," said Jinx. "We thought we'd better get rid of him, so we sneezed a couple of times and rattled things around in the closet, and I guess he thought the chambermaid was in there, because he sneaked right out."

"He got enough," Freddy said; "he got the cape. And he's no fool; he can put two and two together. If anybody's the fool, it's me. I thought by coming here I'd be able to figure out some way of getting him to leave the hotel. But I haven't accomplished anything, and . . ."

"Oh, you're just breaking my heart!" Jinx interrupted sarcastically. "If we hadn't come to the hotel we wouldn't have known that Zingo was going to rob our bank, and he'd have cleaned the place out. We're doing all right. Come on, chief, give 'em the old war whoop. Sharpen up your tomahawk. We'll get Zingo's scalp yet."

"Oh, I'm not giving up," said Freddy, but he didn't say it with much conviction. If Zingo knew who he was, he might as well hang up the Indian suit in the closet and go home. For if he didn't—well, it would be just too bad.

As a matter of fact, it *was* too bad—and no later than that afternoon.

## Chapter 14

So far the watch that the mice and the spiders had been keeping on the magician hadn't turned up anything of value. Of course they had seen and described to Freddy a good many of the gadgets that Zingo used in doing his tricks, and this information was to be valuable later on. They had found about a hundred dollars tucked away in a shoe in a suitcase, but although Freddy was sure this was what was left of the hundred and thirty that Zingo had cheated him out of at the magic show, he wouldn't let them take it. "I'm going to get it back," he said, "but I'm not going to steal it."

One thing they found puzzled them a good deal. It was a little mirror about the size of a ten-cent piece set in a ring. Usually Zingo wore it on his little finger, but once or twice he had left it on the bureau, and there the mice had seen it and wondered about it.

"He's an awful vain man," said Quik. "He's always twisting that little moustache of his. Maybe he wears it so he can admire himself in it."

"He's not that kind of vain," said Cousin Augustus. "He's the kind that doesn't think he ever needs to look in the glass. He thinks he always looks handsome."

"He always wears it with the mirror part turned in, I notice," said Eek.

"I think," said Freddy when they told him about it, "that it's something he uses in his tricks. Skip it; we've got bigger things to worry about."

Freddy stayed in all that morning worrying. Usually there's nothing very constructive about worrying, but Freddy was a good journalist, and he had learned that what can't be helped can sometimes be turned into copy, and that even your troubles can sometimes be made to pay. He wrote a poem about worrying for the next issue of the Bean Home News.

*When life's at its darkest and everything's black,*
*I don't want my friends to come patting my*
    *back.*
*I scorn consolation, can't they let me alone?*
*I just want to snivel, sob, bellow and groan.*

*There's a pleasure in weeping, a joy in despair;*
*There's a great satisfaction in tearing my hair.*
*Don't tell me I'm handsome: I want to be plain;*
*I don't want the sunshine; I want it to rain.*

*Why can't my friends see, when I'm feeling so*
    *low,*
*That the lower I get, then the higher I'll go*
*Later on. For before you can rise, you must*
    *drop;*
*If you haven't hit bottom, you can't reach the*
    *top.*

*For the way to be helpful to those who are down*
*Is not to be merry and act like a clown,*

*But to look on the dark side, and groan, and
    predict
That ruin impends, and they're finally licked.*

*So when I feel awful, just point out my faults,
Don't try to console me and ask me to waltz.
Just tell me I'm stupid, convince me I'm sick,
Assert that my skull is some four inches thick.*

*And then pretty soon when you've got me below
The point where my misery'd normally go,
I'll begin to feel better; I'll shake off my woes,
And I'll haul off and give you a sock on the nose.*

*By which you will know that your duty is done.
It may have been painful—may not have been
    fun;
But though flat on your back with your nose in
    a sling,
You're satisfied, knowing you've done the right
    thing.*

When he had finished he was hungry and he
put on his war bonnet and went down to dinner.

Zingo had evidently finished when Freddy
got into the dining room, for he was sitting in
the lobby with his back to the door, and paid

no attention to the pig. Apparently he didn't see him either when, nearly an hour later, Freddy came out and went off down the street.

"Why does he keep twisting that moustache all the time," Freddy wondered. "Must be nervous. I expect he's very highly strung—all magicians are. So are all pigs, for that matter, but of course pigs don't have moustaches. Rather a pity. Good way to let off extra steam when you're nervous. All I can do is squeal and jump up and down. Though I suppose I could twist my tail. If I could reach it. Might make a poem out of that."

These reflections carried him to the door of the Busy Bee Department Store. He passed several acquaintances as he went down the stairs to the basement, and was relieved when no one recognized him. He bought a few things, and had started up the stairs again when someone brushed by him so closely that he was nearly knocked off his feet.

A woman behind him said indignantly: "Such manners!" He turned to look and saw that it was Signor Zingo who had jostled him. Evidently the magician had been in a hurry and hadn't noticed him at all. But as he turned to go on there was a shout behind him of "Stop, thief! Stop that boy!" and he swung round to see Zingo running towards him, waving his arms excitedly.

"Oh, gosh!" said Freddy. In an instant he was surrounded by a lot of yelling angry people who hustled and snatched at him, while Zingo, holding firmly to his arm, kept shouting: "He stole my billfold! Search his pockets!"

Freddy knew perfectly well that Zingo's billfold would be found in his pocket. He remembered now to have felt a tug at the side of his coat when the magician had pushed past him. He was in a spot, all right. But he could only submit when Mr. Metacarpus, the manager of the Busy Bee, came pushing through the crowd.

Mr. Metacarpus was a tall man who spent most of his time walking through the store, blowing through his big moustache and keeping an eye on the clerks, to see that they didn't slap the customers. For the Busy Bee clerks were a pretty independent crew, and there were a lot of the customers who deserved to be slapped all right. A number of the clerks did too, for that matter. If everybody got what was coming to them, there would be a lot of red cheeks in the big department stores, on both sides of the counter.

Mr. Metacarpus stood in front of Freddy, rubbing his hands and bowing from the waist as if the pig was a customer. Everybody was quiet to hear what he would say. And he said: "What seems to be the trouble?"

Immediately everyone began talking at once. But Mr. Metacarpus was used to that. The motto of the Busy Bee was: "The customer is always right, but never admit it." And so in the store there were a good many disputes between clerks and customers that Mr. Metacarpus had to settle. Experience had taught him that the quickest way to settle one was to get the person that made the most noise and the one that said the least together in his office and thrash the question out. So as Signor Zingo was just about shouting his head off, and Freddy wasn't saying anything at all, he said: "If you gentlemen will just come into my office . . ."

Mr. Metacarpus and Signor Zingo and Freddy went into the office and shut the door, and Mr. Metacarpus searched Freddy. And he found, not only Zingo's billfold, but three neckties and a harmonica and four candy bars and a bottle of hair tonic. All of these things had the store's pricemark on them. Signor Zingo had certainly done a thorough job.

Mr. Metacarpus blew through his moustache and said: "Terrible! Terrible! Such a thing hasn't happened in the Busy Bee in all the years I have been managing it. What is your name, you little villain?"

"He's old Groper's nephew, at the hotel," said Zingo quickly. "Pretty young to be a pickpocket, but I expect Groper has trained him."

"Groper wouldn't do that," said Mr. Metacarpus. "Oh, no; why I went to school with Ollie Groper!"

"What is that supposed to prove?" said Zingo contemptuously. "I went to school with Ed Flaggett, who's doing ten years for highway robbery, but does that prove I'm a crook?"

"But you *are* a crook," said Freddy. "You planted those things in my pocket. When you went downstairs and . . ."

Smack! Zingo's hand slapped Freddy's cheek hard. "Shut up, you miserable little thief! Well, Mr. Manager, are you going to call the police?"

Mr. Metacarpus was pretty nearsighted or he would certainly have recognized Freddy, for although they were not friends, he knew the pig by sight. He reached for the phone. "Oh, I suppose so. Couldn't we just give him a licking and let him go? He's pretty young to go to jail."

*"What seems to be the trouble?"*

Zingo appeared to give this some thought. "Why, I don't want to be too hard on him . . . I wonder . . . How would it be if I just gave him a good talking to? After all, I've got my billfold and you've got your goods. Suppose you just leave me alone with him here for a while?"

Mr. Metacarpus said perhaps that would be the best thing, and went out and shut the door.

Zingo's manner changed at once. He smiled his meanest smile. "Well, my friend, so you thought you could put something over on Zingo, eh? And now Zingo's got you, like *that*!" He reached out and gave Freddy a vicious pinch.

Freddy sat still. He was pretty sure he could lick Zingo in a fair fight, but he couldn't lick Mr. Metacarpus and everybody in the Busy Bee, and that is what he would have to do to get away. But he added it up in his mind: two pinches and a slap. He would send in his bill for those some day, with interest.

"You thought I didn't know you, I suppose, because I didn't look at you very closely," Zingo went on. "But I've been watching you when you didn't know it; I've got eyes in the back of my head, pig."

Freddy didn't say anything.

"And don't count on your friend the sheriff

—we've caught you with the goods, and he'll have to arrest you and put you in jail for a good long time." Zingo stopped smiling. "You stupid, fat pig!" he snarled. "You and those silly animals, all puffed up with pride and dumbness! To think you could fool *me!*—me who have fooled doctors and lawyers, kings and school-teachers and major generals!" He went on and made quite a speech about himself.

Freddy still didn't say anything.

At last Zingo stopped. He walked to the window and stood looking out, with his back to Freddy, fingering his moustache, and Freddy caught the glitter of the little mirror on his ring. "I'll make a deal with you," he said. "Give me back my hat and I'll let you go."

Freddy said: "Give me what you've got left of that hundred and thirty dollars you skinned me out of, and I'll give it back."

"You're in no position to bargain," said Zingo. "Give it back or go to jail."

"I don't mind going to jail," said Freddy. "It's a nice jail. I spend a lot of time there anyway."

Zingo shrugged. "I won that money fairly," he said. "But I don't want to be hard on you. I'll give you back fifty of it."

There was something pretty funny about this, Freddy thought. Why was Zingo so anxious to get the hat back? It was just an ordinary silk hat with a trick lining; Zingo could get another one made for much less than fifty dollars. There could be only one answer: something of value was concealed in the hat. Something small, something that Presto certainly knew about . . . He said: "All right. I'll go get the hat now."

So Zingo went out and spoke to Mr. Metacarpus and they let Freddy go. "But if you're not back before supper with the hat," the magician said, "we'll have the state troopers as well as the sheriff on your trail. So I wouldn't try to hide or run away."

But Freddy had no intention of running away. He trotted straight out to the farm. At the bank he got the hat up from the vault and examined it. At first he could find nothing in it. The secret compartment in the top was quite empty. But under the lining, on one side it seemed to be just a trifle thicker. He loosened a few of the stitches and there underneath, pasted to the side of the hat, was an envelope. He got it out. In it were nine fifty-dollar bills.

Unquestionably that was part of the money

Zingo had stolen from Mr. Boomschmidt—the part Presto said the magician had lost. And of course he *had* lost it, when the hat blew away. "This explains a lot of things," said Freddy, and he left the money in the vault and trotted back to Centerboro with the hat.

It would be foolish to trust Zingo to carry out his side of the bargain. He certainly wouldn't carry it out if he knew that the money was gone. So Freddy went first to the Busy Bee and got Mr. Metacarpus to go with him to the hotel, where they found Signor Zingo in the lobby. The magician didn't dare to look in the hat for the money in front of Mr. Metacarpus. But he took the hat with him when he went up to his room to get the fifty dollars he had promised Freddy.

"Well," said Mr. Metacarpus, "I must be getting back." He looked severely at Freddy and blew out his moustache, pooff, as if to get it out of the way of what he was about to say. "I hope, young man, that this will be a lesson to you. You have escaped a severe and well-deserved punishment only through the generosity of Signor Zingo. I hope you are properly grateful. I hope you realize," said Mr. Metacarpus, "that crime does not pay."

"I wish you could make Zingo realize that," Freddy said. "I didn't steal those things; he planted them on me. He's a sleight of hand performer—it was easy for him. But please don't go till he comes back. I want a witness here."

Mr. Metacarpus blew his moustache out, then sucked it in, then blew it out again. "I don't understand all this," he said. "What is this hat? Where did you get it? It is all very confusing."

At that moment Signor Zingo appeared at the head of the stairs. He looked very much upset; his hands were closing and unclosing nervously and when he called to Freddy it was plain that he was refraining from some very bad language only with the greatest difficulty. "You—boy! Come here! Come up here a minute!"

"You come down," said Freddy calmly.

"Come up!" said Zingo. "I want to—I want to speak to you. Come up and get your reward."

"You give it to me right here," said Freddy firmly.

"OK," shouted Zingo, suddenly losing all control of his temper. "I will!" And he made a dash down the stairs.

His intention of beating up Freddy was so plain that Mr. Metacarpus put a protecting hand on the pig's shoulder. "Come, come, sir," he said, "no disturbance, I beg. If you have any complaint to make . . ."

Freddy saw no point in staying around the hotel any longer. He was out in the street in two seconds and running for his life. Although he was still in the Indian suit, he had to run on all fours really to make time, and it surprised an awful lot of passers-by to see what they thought was a little boy in fringed leggings and a war bonnet galloping up the middle of the street like a four-footed animal with a magician in pursuit. Several older people got so confused by the sight that they shouted: "Runaway! Runaway!" and tried to stop him. But Freddy dodged them successfully, and soon left Zingo far behind.

## Chapter 15

Freddy made straight for the jail. Some of the prisoners were playing croquet, and they waved their mallets and called to him to join them, but he only waved back and went on in to the sheriff's office. The sheriff was just hanging up the phone, and he said: "Hello, Freddy. Been talking to Ollie Groper. He's kind of disappointed in you, I guess."

"Well," said Freddy, "I don't blame him. But if I'd had you arrest Zingo, you'd have had him as a prisoner here, and I knew you wouldn't like that. Anyway, I didn't want him to be locked up, because then he couldn't give his show Tuesday night, and I've got some plans about that. After the show I'll figure out some way of getting him out of the hotel. But right now I've discovered something pretty important." And he told his friend about the money he had found in Zingo's hat.

"H'm," said the sheriff, "you'd better write Boomschmidt about it. I see by the paper the circus is in Binghamton this week; he could drive up and get his money. Hey, did you see this?" He pawed around on his desk until he found the Binghamton paper, which he folded and handed to Freddy.

"Well, well," said the pig. " 'Boomschmidt's Stupendous and . . .' Yes, it's the same ad he always uses. But what's this?—'The Great Bald African Lion. Only specimen of this gigantic and ferocious animal ever captured alive.' My goodness, do you suppose that's Leo? 'The bald lion bears the same relation to other lions that the great American bald eagle does to other eagles. Captured at immense cost and at the peril of his life by Orestes Boomschmidt, in person, on the South African veldt. Mr. Boomschmidt enters the cage twice daily.' Oh sure, that's Leo, with his mane clipped. But I wonder how they manage it. Leo doesn't like to be locked up. But if they're pretending he's so ferocious, they can't let him run around loose and call on his friends the way he used to do."

"Look, Freddy," said the sheriff; "the hotel isn't a very safe place for you. This Zingo is a tough egg—too tough for you to handle. I know you're smart, and you've tangled with some bad characters in the past, but he'd shoot you as soon as look at you. I don't know what you've got up your sleeve for Tuesday night, but my advice to you is: drop it. I know he stuck you for a lot of money. But it isn't worth risking your life to get it back."

But Freddy shook his head. It wasn't the money—he could afford to lose that; it was his professional pride. Zingo had put one over on him; he had to get even. And there was Mr. Groper. He had promised Mr. Groper his help, but so far he had accomplished nothing.

They argued for a while but Freddy was firm, and at last the sheriff said: "Well, at least come stay here until after the show."

"I'll stay here tonight," said Freddy. "Then we'll see."

So Freddy played croquet with Maxie the Yegg until suppertime, and after supper he entertained the prisoners with some magic. But at nine o'clock he got up and said he had to go out for a while. The sheriff looked worried but didn't try to stop him. Freddy went down to the hotel and went in through the kitchen and up the back stairs. But as his head came above the level of the top step so that he could see down the hall, he stopped. For light streamed from the open door of Zingo's room, and Zingo himself sat in a chair in the doorway. He had a heavy cane in his hand, and it didn't take much detective ability to deduce what he was waiting for.

Freddy ducked down. And he was wondering what he had better do when something tickled his nose, and he felt the very smallest of small footsteps walking up towards his ear. "Webb!" he whispered. "I'd know that walk anywhere! What goes on here?"

"We've been waiting to drop on you if you came up—mother at the front stairs, and me here," said Mr. Webb. "As far as we can make out, from what Zingo and Presto have been saying, you took something out of Zingo's hat. He thinks you hid it somewhere, and he's laying for you, and if he catches you he's going to make you tell where it is. He said he'd beat you till you told him."

"My goodness," said Freddy, "I'm glad you stopped me. Has anything else happened?"

"Ain't that enough?" said Mr. Webb. "Well, yes; Old Whibley came to the window a while ago. He had a pistol for you or something. Jinx offered to give it to you but Whibley wouldn't let him have it—said nobody but a fool would trust a cat with firearms. He'll be back in half an hour or so."

"Well," Freddy said, "we've got to change our headquarters to the theatre. Tell Jinx and Minx to pack my suitcase and throw it out the window. Then they and the mice can sneak out this way. I don't think Zingo will notice them, and it won't matter if he does. You'd better collect Mrs. Webb and ride along. I'll meet you at the back door of the theatre—on the alley, you know—at ten o'clock."

The second show was about half over when Freddy reached the back door of the theatre, which Mr. Muszkiski always kept unlocked until the show was over, in case of fire. His friends were waiting for him—even the beetles and caterpillars, who with the Webbs had ridden on Minx's back. "It was a cinch, Freddy," said Jinx. "Zingo heard your window go up when we hove the suitcase out, and he ran to *his* window to see what the row was about. And while he was there we unlocked the door and got out without his seeing us. So now what do we do?"

"We go down and camp in one of those rooms under the stage," said Freddy, "and get ready for Tuesday night."

Old Whibley had evidently been watching when they left the hotel, for now he swept down and lit on the eaves trough over the door. "Hey! You!" he hooted. "You'd better have this." And Zingo's pistol thumped down at Freddy's feet.

The pig picked it up. "Oh, thank you!"

"Would have let you have it before, but I wanted to try it out," said the owl. "Figured if I could get the hang of the thing, 'twould simplify hunting. As it is now, I don't have time to keep up to date in my thinking—have to spend it all hunting. If I could go out and pot a couple of field mice in the early evening—"

"You big cannibal!" squeaked Cousin Augustus angrily, and Eek sniffed. "Such talk!"

Whibley gave his hooting laugh. "Don't worry about me, you scrawny little things," he said. "House mice! Got no more flavor than something out of the dust pan! Now a good field mouse . . ."

"Did you shoot any?" Freddy asked.

"Guess I need practice," said the owl. "Only had six shots in the gun, and missed every time. But you can get some more cartridges. And I'd like the pistol back after you've plugged Zingo. Know how to use it?" And when Freddy said he didn't, Whibley said: "Glad I won't be around while you're learning. Don't want to get a claw shot off."

"Well, I guess I can equal your score anyway," said Freddy. "Six misses in six shots—I ought to be able to do as well as that."

Whibley clattered his beak angrily, but apparently couldn't think of any comeback, and Freddy said quickly: "Excuse me—I don't mean to be rude. Will you be around to help us out Tuesday night?"

"Can't promise," said the owl. "As I told you, I'm way back in my thinking. Pshaw!" he said. "I'm not catching up with it talking to you." And he flew off.

When they were inside, Eek said: "Do owls do so much thinking, usually?"

"They *say* they do," Jinx replied contemptuously. "Personally I think all their talk about being so wise is a lot of whoosh. It takes more than a pair of big eyes and a bad disposition to set up in the wisdom business."

"Whibley's wise all right," Freddy said. "And he'll be around, no matter what he says. He always comes through."

With headquarters now established in the dressing room under the stage at the movie theatre, Freddy and his friends kept under cover for the next two days. On Monday Zingo had his magic paraphernalia moved from the hotel over to the theatre, and when he had checked the stuff over and had gone, the animals came out of hiding and went to work on it.

"Boy," said Eeny, emerging from one of the secret pockets of the magician's tail coat, "old Zing is going to be surprised at the way some of his tricks come out; eh, Freddy?"

"I hope so," said Freddy. "We've sure put some extra magic in some of them. But he's a smart magician; I hope he doesn't turn the tables on us. I still don't know how he spotted who I was. It must have been when I was in the hotel dining room, but I kept my face pretty well hidden by the war bonnet, and I didn't eat anything—I mean so he'd see I had trotters instead of hands—except when his back was turned. He said he had eyes in the back of his head, and I guess it's so."

Late in the afternoon Freddy went over to the jail. He didn't dare wear the Indian suit, or to be seen on the street just as himself either, so he wore the old woman disguise, with a shawl over his head, that he had used successfully several times before. He wanted to see if anything had been heard of Mr. Boomschmidt, and sure enough, just as he was going in the gate a horn blared behind him, and he jumped aside as a big red and gold car, with a B surmounted by a crown painted on the door, swept past him up the drive. Bill Wonks was driving, and side by side in the back seat sat Mr. Boomschmidt and Leo. Leo had on a pair of sun glasses, he leaned back against the cushions looking very haughty and noble and relaxed, but the thing that startled Freddy was his mane. It was long and hung down in ringlets on each side of his face; and it was a sort of pinkish orange.

Freddy giggled under his breath, then pulled the shawl around his face and hurried after them. He came up just as they were getting out of the car.

"Ah, ye wretches," he wailed at them; "steal-

*He leaned back against the cushions looking very haughty.*

in' up behind in your great roarin' engine and scarin' a poor widdy woman out of her boots! Think shame to yourselves, ye rich and haughty misters! Ridin' around the country in your plug hats and your moth-eaten wigs, and laughin' and roarin' when you run over a poor old helpless body like meself, and if me dear husband, Patrick O'Halloran, was alive, the saints be with him, he'd have the teeth out of ye and you layin' on your faces bawlin' for mercy. But I'll have the law on ye, so I will, or my name's not . . ."

Mr. Boomschmidt interrupted him with a shout. "Your husband was Pat O'Halloran? Dear old Pat O'Halloran, that used to be—"

"He used to be nothin' that you're about to say he used to be," Freddy cut in. He knew that this was always Mr. Boomschmidt's method of avoiding an argument. He would pick on some minor detail and get everyone so mixed up that they forgot what they were arguing about. "And anyway," the pig went on, "it's not you I'm addressin', me good man, but this long-tailed refugee from a mothball factory, this . . ."

"Easy now, lady," said Leo, taking off his sun glasses. "Why, dye my hair," he exclaimed, staring at Freddy, "aren't you the Mrs. O'Halloran that used to live on—now let me see, what street was it? I've heard some nice things about you. I—"

"Have ye, indeed?" said Freddy. "Well, I've heard some things about you, come to see who you are, for I'm that Mrs. O'Halloran that you stole the leg of lamb from last time ye was through, the two of ye was in it." He turned to appeal to the sheriff, who had come out to welcome his guests. "Arrest them, sheriff, the two villains. 'Twas them that broke into me house and grabbed me and the little one there sat on me head while the other ransacked me cupboard and stole a leg of lamb and off they run the two of them and . . ."

"Wait a minute, *wait* a minute!" said the sheriff calmly. "We'll go inside and talk it over, ma'am. In with you," and he caught Freddy's arm and dragged him inside, while Mr. Boomschmidt and Leo followed, looking puzzled but not very much disturbed.

"Goodness gracious, sheriff!" Mr. Boomschmidt said. "Glad to buy this lady a leg of lamb if she wants it. Buy her all four legs if she says so, and two quarts of mint sauce to go with 'em. Hire her to write my advertising, too, if

she's willing. My, my, such wonderful language
—eh, Leo? Fugitive from a mothball factory,
why it's a gift, that's what it is, a gift!"

"If you say so, chief," said Leo grumpily.

"Well I do say so," Mr. Boomschmidt replied. "Look at what she called you for nothing,
and imagine what she could think up if she was
paid for it."

"Ye'll not have to pay me!" Freddy said. "It's
no trouble at all at all with a face like that to
embroider me thoughts on, and an old floor mop
tied on the top of it the way the prisoners here
would go into roarin' hysterics if it was stuck
in the door at them." He stopped suddenly, for
Leo, with a swift swipe of his paw had snatched
off the shawl.

"Well, boil my wig!" said Leo. "I thought
there was something familiar about that figure.
Little stouter, ain't you, Freddy?"

"Upon my soul," said Mr. Boomschmidt,
"I'd have known that poetical language anywhere. I mean, I'd have known it was you
anywhere, Freddy—if I hadn't known it wasn't."

"But it was, chief," said Leo.

"Sure," said Mr. Boomschmidt, "that's what
I mean."

"Look, Mr. Boomschmidt," said Freddy; "I

suppose you've come up for that money? It's up in our bank. Shall we go out and get it?"

"No hurry. We're staying over to see the show tomorrow night, if the sheriff can put us up. We don't want to go to the hotel, on account of Zingo."

"You mean *you* don't, chief," said Leo. "Can you beat it, Freddy? Guess why the boss doesn't want to see Zingo: because it might hurt Zingo's feelings to run into somebody he'd stolen money from!"

"Well, good gracious, I can't help it; I can't *help* it, Leo," said Mr. Boomschmidt, sounding a little irritated. "I know you say it's super-sensitive and silly, but oh my goodness, it would make me uncomfortable and I won't do it!"

Freddy changed the subject. "Look, Leo; there's something I don't understand. According to the Binghamton paper you're billed as the Great Bald African Lion. But why the pink wig?"

"Wrong color, isn't it?" said Leo distastefully. "Pink and tawny yellow are a horrible color combination—you needn't tell me, I know it. But it was all I could get in Binghamton—can you imagine?—not a single artificial lion mane in the whole burg. I found a beauty shop, and they made this up—it was this or platinum blonde, and I thought this was—well, more suitable, somehow."

"But why wear one at all?"

"Oh, good gracious," put in Mr. Boom-schmidt, "I couldn't have him running around the fair grounds out of his cage when he was billed as the most ferocious animal in the whole Dark Continent, could I? When I'm supposed to be risking my life every time I enter his cage. We've had wonderful attendance in Bingham-ton—wonderful. People all coming and bring-ing their kids in the hope of seeing me torn to pieces. Wouldn't have much hope of that if they'd just seen him having a coke at the soda fountain ten minutes before, would they? So he wears this mane outside the cage."

"I see," said Freddy. "Well, come on; let's go out and get that money."

## Chapter 16

The curtain rose Tuesday evening before what the Bean Home News later described as "the most distinguished animal audience—not to speak of the prominent humans—ever gathered together in the fair city of Centerboro." All of those who had attended Freddy's performance were there, and many others—some drawn by the fame of Signor Zingo, others by the rumor that Freddy intended to expose the magician's tricks and thus win back the money he had lost

on his own show. There were even two cows
and a horse who had walked all the way over
from Tushville.

Signor Zingo, in his tall silk hat and his red-
lined cape, twirled his moustache and smiled in
gratification as he stood in the center of the
stage and looked out upon the rows and rows
of faces that were turned towards him. He
might not have smiled so confidently if he had
known that there were several dozen of Freddy's
friends concealed in various parts of the theatre,
ready to take parts in his performance which he
had not assigned to them. Or if he had seen the
short round man in a plug hat and the very large
and queerly shaped lady with a mop of pinkish
orange hair only partly tied down to her head
by a large scarf, and with fingernails four inches
long, who slipped into the back row just after
the lights in the house went down.

On the previous evening, after Mr. Boomschmidt had collected his money from the First
Animal Bank and, with Leo, had gone in to
pay a short call on the Beans, Freddy had got
together all the animals who were to help him
at the show, and the big red car had taken them
back to the theatre. Tuesday morning Freddy
had drilled them in what they had to do, and

then they had gone to their positions where they stayed till the show began.

From the reports of the mice, who had watched Zingo practicing and had heard him discussing his tricks with Presto, Freddy had got a pretty good idea of just how the program was to go, and he had made elaborate preparations. When the curtain went up, Zingo had planned to step forward, wave his magic wand, and produce presumably from nowhere a large bouquet of paper flowers which he would present with a pretty speech to some lady in the front row.

The wand, of course, was hollow, and the bouquet, folded very tightly, was inside it. But although Zingo waved the wand gracefully several times and commanded the flowers to appear, nothing happened. For Freddy had poured a little glue into the wand.

Zingo however was quickwitted enough to produce from a secret pocket a couple of little silk flags, and he made it appear that these were what he had expected, and he leaned down and presented them to Mrs. Bean and Mrs. Weezer, who sat side by side in the first row. But the applause was rather lukewarm.

The second trick was called "The Dancing Cane." Zingo balanced a cane upright on the floor in front of him, and then without touching it, he moved his hands about it, and the cane danced and jigged all by itself. It was a good trick, and everyone had started to clap, when down the aisle came Freddy. He had on his war bonnet, but instead of the Indian suit, he wore his own magician's coat with the secret pockets and clips.

He stopped just below the stage and said in a loud voice: "I claim the ten dollars you offer to anyone who can duplicate or explain any of your tricks, Signor Zingo."

Zingo scowled ferociously at him, but Freddy climbed up on the stage and showed how by means of black threads, which the audience of course couldn't see, and which were looped around the cane and fastened at the ends to the magician's fingers, he could make the cane dance.

Zingo showed a thin line of white teeth in a tight smile. "Very good," he said. "Very clever of you. I will instruct the box office to pay you ten dollars when you leave the theatre."

But Freddy shook his head. "You were going to give me fifty dollars when I brought back your hat," he said, "and I haven't seen that yet. Under the circumstances, I prefer the cash to a promise." Zingo didn't dare refuse. He sent Presto out to the box office for the money, and Freddy waited until it was handed to him before he stepped down.

But as he was leaving the stage Zingo stopped him. With a hand on Freddy's arm he turned to the audience. "You will remember, ladies and gentlemen," he said, "that last week when I accepted the challenge of my young colleague here to explain his tricks, I did not demand immediate payment in cash when I exposed his rather childish mystifications. But I will ask you to excuse his bad manners, ladies and gentlemen, for he is very young and very suspicious. And to show you that I am not offended by what some might call downright boorishness, I am going to ask him to remain on the stage during the rest of the performance. I wish to give him every opportunity to observe my work, and if he can duplicate or explain my effects, I will be only too happy to stand by the terms of my offer."

A murmur of sympathy for the magician came from the audience, and Freddy felt that he had lost some ground with them. A few of his friends knew of the mean tricks Zingo had played on him, but those who knew nothing of

Zingo's real character felt that his performance was being interfered with.

Freddy knew that he looked ridiculous in his feathered war bonnet and plaid coat; he knew that Zingo's purpose in asking him to remain on the stage was to make the audience laugh at him; and he suspected that the magician would try to make him look a complete fool by playing tricks on him. But Freddy also had some tricks up his sleeve—or rather concealed among the eagle feathers of his headdress and in the secret pockets of his coat. And, what was better than all his tricks, Freddy had the ability to keep his temper. He knew that he had the advantage of Zingo there. For in a fight, or in a contest of any kind, the one who keeps his temper has an advantage that is equal to two shotguns and a small cannon. And so he just stood back and waited.

Zingo came down to the front of the stage. He stood there, twirling his moustache, just smiling at the audience. Freddy reached up and adjusted his war bonnet more firmly on his head. And immediately, without turning round, Zingo said: "Perhaps you'd be more comfortable if you took that headdress off, chief."

The audience laughed and wondered how

Zingo had known what Freddy was doing; and Freddy wondered too. Zingo had his back turned; he was facing the darkened auditorium —there was no mirror . . ."Mirror!" thought Freddy. "Oh, golly!" For he suddenly remembered Zingo's ring, with the bit of looking glass mounted in it. The glass that was always on the *inside* of his finger. "That's how he recognized me!" Freddy thought. "When he was twirling his moustache, and had his back turned, he was watching me all the time!"

His first idea was to explain the trick and collect another ten dollars. Then he thought he'd better wait. Zingo did other tricks with that ring—better ones. And anyway, it was a good idea to let Zingo push him around a little first; It would make the audience stop feeling quite so sorry for the magician.

After a minute Zingo turned and looked at him. And then he began laughing. He stared and laughed and pointed at Freddy; he slapped his knees and guffawed. Still shaking with laughter, he led Freddy to the front of the stage and bending over him, peered down into the circle of feathers that made up the top part of the war bonnet. "My goodness, chief," he said, "don't you ever comb your hair?" He reached

in and apparently pulled out a number of objects which he held up one by one, then threw
on the stage—three pieces of coal, an old bird's
nest, and four or five old chicken bones. "Very
untidy," he said. "Very bad manners to come
before an audience without cleaning up a little
beforehand."

"I'm sorry," said Freddy, "but I thought a
magician had to be sort of grubby. Of course
I've never seen any magician but you, and you
can't blame me, when you're so sloppy."

Zingo's grin faded and he said sharply: "What
do you mean, I'm sloppy?"

"Well," said Freddy, "would you just let me
take that hat a minute?"

"Certainly not!" said Zingo, pulling away.
But voices in the audience shouted: "Aw, let
him have it!" "Give it to him!" "Very well,"
said Zingo reluctantly, "but be careful of it—
it's a very expensive hat, and if you—" He
stopped abruptly, for Freddy had taken the hat,
reached into it, and pulled out a mouse, two
caterpillars and three beetles, which he held up
one by one, as Zingo had, and then set down on
the table.

"I leave it to you, ladies and gentlemen," he
said, "which of us is the more careless about

*"My goodness, Chief . . ."*

combing his hair. But there's something else here," he went on. He reached in the hat again and brought out three teaspoons. He looked at the handles. "H'm," he said, "Centerboro Hotel. That's where you stay, isn't it? Mr. Groper told me he'd been missing a lot of cutlery lately. H'm, let's see if there's any more stolen property here."

He reached in the hat, but Zingo snatched it away from him. "That's enough of this," he said. "Let's get on with the show."

Freddy moved back and leaned against the table, so that his confederates—the mouse and the caterpillars and beetles—could crawl back into his pockets without being noticed, and Zingo picked up a pack of cards and began to do sleight-of-hand tricks with them. He got Mr. Bean and Mr. Rohr up on the stage and had them pick out cards, or even just think of them, and the cards they had picked would fly up out of the pack or be found in their pockets, or he would throw the pack in the air and all the other cards would fall face down, but the one they had chosen would fall face up. He did a lot of very clever card manipulation, and Freddy couldn't explain any of it. But at last he did a trick that Freddy caught on to.

Mr. Rohr took the cards, shuffled them thoroughly, then handed them one by one, face down, to Zingo, who passed them right on to Mr. Bean. And as he passed them on he would name each one—jack of diamonds, two of spades, and so on—and Mr. Bean would look at them. Each time Zingo was right.

"I claim another ten dollars," said Freddy. "I can explain that trick."

"Oh, go away," said Zingo. "You're interrupting the performance."

"Come, come, sir," said Mr. Rohr. "Play fair, sir; play fair."

So Zingo had to stand by while Freddy explained about the ring with the mirror set in it. "You see," he said, "the mirror is on the inside of his finger, and it reflects the face of each card as he hands it to Mr. Bean."

So Zingo had to send Presto out for another ten dollars.

Now a good magic performance takes a lot of preparation. Each secret pocket in the magician's coat must contain one or more articles which are to be made to appear later. Colored silk handkerchiefs, folding bird cages, fish bowls—there is no end to the things that can be concealed by a clever performer. But under Freddy's instructions, the mice had given Zingo's coat a good working over. They had done a lot of gnawing on it. They had gnawed the seams so that they were just held together by one or two threads, and they had gnawed the pockets partly through, so that at the slightest strain everything in them would fall out. And to be sure that everything *did* fall out at the proper time, one of the beetles, who had exceptionally strong jaws, had volunteered for the dangerous job of concealing himself in one of the pockets and snipping the last threads after the performance began. The mice had also loosened buttons, and chewed through the elastic "pulls," fastened inside the sleeves to make objects disappear. Cousin Augustus had had two front teeth loosened when one of these elastics snapped back on him when he was cutting it.

So now as Zingo went on with his performance, things began to happen to him. The first was when several things refused to vanish when he commanded them to. He covered up the failure cleverly, making them disappear by sleight-of-hand with his nimble fingers. But the tricks didn't go smoothly and the audience didn't applaud.

Then a glass pitcher fell through one weakened pocket and crashed to the floor. "I can explain that trick," said Freddy. "There's a hole in your pocket." But he didn't claim ten dollars.

Zingo was too experienced to show anger, or the dismay that he must have felt. He tried to turn it off by saying to Freddy: "You quit throwing crockery at me or you'll have to leave the stage."

Then things began really to go wrong. Presto brought a sword from the back of the stage and with a bow presented it to Zingo, who began making passes with it in the air. At the tip of the sword would appear after one pass a string of colored lights, after another, a bouquet of flowers. Freddy didn't know how this was done, but he was sure that if Zingo continued to jump about so actively something would happen. And it did. First several buttons popped off the magician's vest and rattled on the floor; then, as he turned for a moment from the audience to sweep the sword high in the air, the back of his coat split from collar to tail. Another pocket gave way and three eggs fell and broke, a pair of handcuffs dropped from somewhere, followed by a shower of smaller articles.

Zingo threw down the sword in a rage. His face was purple with mortification and his teeth glinted in an angry snarl as he came down to the footlights, his split coat flapping ridiculously. He started to say something, then seemed to lose all control of his temper, for he whirled about, snatched up the sword and charged straight at Freddy.

## Chapter 17

Now Freddy had exposed only two tricks so far, and had got back only twenty of his hundred and thirty dollars. But he was having an awfully good time. And yet as he stood and watched Zingo's performance go to pieces, he couldn't help feeling a little sorry for the magician. Zingo was a crook; he had stolen from Freddy and cheated and abused him; and yet Freddy had begun to feel that he wanted to help him.

Some people would think this was pretty weak of Freddy, and others would say that it was simply good sportsmanship not to jump on an enemy when he was down. You'll have to decide that for yourself. Anyway, Freddy didn't feel like that very long. When Zingo started for him with the sword Freddy ducked around behind the table, and pulled out the magician's pistol. "Stop!" he shouted, "or I'll shoot!"

Of course the pistol was empty, but Zingo didn't know that. "Go ahead and shoot!" he said, but he stopped.

About the only way anybody could ever tell if Freddy was scared was when his tail came uncurled. When he was gay and on top of the world it was curled up as tight as a watch spring, but when he was depressed or frightened all the curl came right out of it. It was uncurled now. But nobody in the audience knew it because it was hidden by his coat. He said: "Stand right where you are, Signor Zingo. I'm going to hypnotize you."

Zingo sneered. "Don't make me laugh!" he said. "Pointing a loaded gun at anybody isn't hypnotizing them!" He half turned towards the audience. "Hypnotism, ladies and gentlemen," he said, "is like mind-reading and escaping from locked trunks. It is only done by the most experienced and accomplished magicians. I may say that I am a skilled performer in all those branches of the black art. It is simply laughable to think that this stupid pig could know anything of such things." He paused a moment, then he said: "I know that he is a neighbor of many of you; you feel a pardonable pride in the cleverness which, I am told, he has shown as a detective. I have no quarrel with that. But he should stick to his detective work, and not venture into a field of which he knows nothing. As a magician, ladies and gentlemen, I assure you that he is clumsy and stupid, and I propose to show him up once for all." He turned to Freddy, and laying the sword on the table and folding his arms, said: "All right; go on and hypnotize me."

Freddy hesitated. "I suppose you think I can't!" he said.

Zingo grinned. "I know you can't, my silly friend."

But there was still something Freddy wanted to get from Zingo before he put the matter to a trial, so he pretended to be rather uncertain. "Well now," he said hesitantly, "if you . . . that is, if I can make you feel pain in any part of your body I point at, will that convince you?"

"Sure, sure," said the magician, becoming

more and more confident. "That will certainly convince me. If you can do that, I'll . . ."

"Will you hand me that fifty dollars you promised to give me for your hat?" Freddy said quickly.

Zingo hesitated, and his eyes narrowed. Then he grinned again, for he was certain that Freddy was bluffing. "Sure," he said again. "Go ahead. You give me a pain in the neck anyway—let's see if you can improve on it."

"O K.," said Freddy. "I'll give you a real pain in the neck." He made a few passes with his arms, and under his breath he whispered: "All right, Jacob. When I point, do your stuff." Then he threw one arm out straight and pointed at Zingo. "You have a terrible pain in the back of your neck!" he shouted.

And immediately Zingo gave a loud yell, crouched down, and seized the back of his neck with both hands.

Only a few of Freddy's friends in the audience had any idea what he was up to. The rest merely saw that they were witnessing a contest between two magicians, which was of course a great deal more exciting to watch than a regular magic performance, and they had sat spellbound. But when it was evident that Freddy really had given

*"You have a terrible pain in the back of your neck!" he shouted.*

Zingo a pain just by pointing at him, they stood up and shouted and cheered. They hadn't even seen Jacob.

Now Jacob was a friend of Freddy's, a slim and elegant black and yellow wasp, who lived with his large family in a sort of apartment house made out of grey paper under the eaves of the cow barn. He and his two younger brothers, Eph and Fritz, had been hidden in the feathers of the war bonnet. They had sat around during the first part of the performance, polishing their stings, and giggling over what they would do to Zingo when Freddy said "Go!" When Freddy whispered, Jacob took off and circled up to gain height; and then when Freddy pointed, he dove. With all four wings humming he shot straight down so fast that none of the audience could have seen him even if they had been looking for him, and he drove his sting into Zingo's neck just above the collar.

"That's for the time you slapped me," said Freddy.

But there were still two pinches to be avenged. He whispered: "Now, Eph!" made a few magic passes, and flung his arm out straight, pointing at the magician's knee. Eph circled up, dove, and Zingo gave a second yell, louder than the first, and his hands, which had been clawing at the back of his neck, flew to his knee. He danced around the stage, now bending forward as he rubbed his knee, now backward as he grabbed at his neck. And Freddy pointed again and Fritz whirred down and stung him on the nose.

The third sting completed Zingo's defeat. Yelling like a banshee he ran twice around the stage, flapping his arms and dodging further imaginary attack, his coat and vest, whose seams had now given out entirely under the strain, fluttering about him. Then he dashed behind the scenes. And Freddy came forward and said: "Ladies and gentlemen, do you agree with me that I won the fifty dollars fairly?"

A shout of "Yes! You won!" went up from the audience.

But Presto, who had followed his master back stage, came out and held up one paw for silence. Signor Zingo, he announced, had something to say; he would return in a moment.

It was more than a moment before Zingo re-appeared, and the audience began to get restless. They whistled and imitated cats and dogs and then they began all stamping in unison and chanting: "Give—Freddy—his money! Give—

Freddy—his money!" I think it was Judge Willey who started it.

But at last Zingo came out. He had covered the wreck of his coat with his long red-lined cape, and he had on his silk hat, and he looked very dignified and impressive except for his nose, which was now a good two sizes too large for his face. He said: "Ladies and gentlemen, I have been the victim of a cruel and malicious trick. I do not admit that I was hypnotized. I was stung by hornets. And to prove this, I will ask a committee of any three gentlemen to come up on the stage and examine my nose and the back of my neck. Now if you will come up, sir—" he pointed to Mr. Metacarpus—"and you—"

"Just a minute," said Freddy. "This is all unnecessary. You all heard Signor Zingo say that he would be convinced that he had been hypnotized if I made him feel pain in the part of his body I pointed at. I submit, my friends, that I did just that. Therefore—"

"It was a trick!" said Zingo angrily.

"Everything you do on this stage is a trick." Freddy retorted. "When you pick a bouquet of flowers out of the air it is a trick—you don't really pick it out of the air. And so if I did not really hypnotize you—"

The stamping and the chant of "Pay—Freddy —his money!" began again and drowned out his words.

Freddy motioned for silence. "Thank you, my friends," he said. "It is evident to you by this time, if you did not already know it, that there is a feud between Signor Zingo and me. Up to this evening Signor Zingo has had all the best of it. Those of you who were here a week ago tonight will remember that Signor Zingo won a hundred and thirty dollars from me by exposing and duplicating my tricks. Now I am not a professional magician, and I had no intention of making that offer of five dollars for each trick exposed. This rabbit, Presto, made the offer in my name, and though I had not authorized it, I felt I should stand by it.

"That was a trick which Signor Zingo played on me. By another trick he attempted to have me put in jail. Therefore, if I am playing malicious tricks on Signor Zingo tonight, I don't believe there is anybody here who will blame me.

"This whole affair, ladies and gentlemen, is

a contest in trickery. However I wish to be fair. I will make Signor Zingo a sporting proposition. You heard him say that he was a skilled mind reader. Therefore, instead of insisting on his paying me the fifty dollars which you, by your applause, have awarded to me, I will challenge him to a contest in mind reading. I will challenge him to put up, instead of fifty, a hundred dollars, and I will put up a like amount. And the one who in your estimation gives the best mind reading performance will take the money."

Zingo had become wary, and would perhaps have refused, but he realized that in the present mood of the audience a refusal would mean the end of his career as a magician. If he backed down before an amateur magician, and a pig at that, nobody would ever hire him again. He laughed shortly. "I accept," he said; "and if that pig can put on a mind-reading performance, I'll eat my hat." And he sent Presto out to the box office for the money.

Freddy, although he was really wealthy for a pig, had no such sum in his pockets. He went down the runway into the aisle and said: "Will anyone here lend me a hundred dollars for half an hour?" Zingo sniggered, but then he gasped, for almost at once handfuls of bills were reached towards Freddy from all directions.

Freddy was pretty pleased at such a response, but as he hesitated which handful to take, Mr. Bean got up from his seat in the front row and came out into the aisle. "You're my pig," he said gruffly. "You take my money, and nobody else's." And after digging down in a pocket which from the trouble he had must have been about two feet deep, he pulled out a huge roll of bills, peeled off five twenties, and stuffed them into Freddy's pocket.

Then Mr. Weezer held the stakes and the mind-reading contest began.

## Chapter 18

Signor Zingo had a very good mind-reading performance of the standard kind. He sat on the stage with the lights on in the house, and Presto went up and down the aisles, taking objects that people handed to him and asking the magician to describe them. He would take, for instance, a watch, and standing with his back to the stage would ask Zingo questions about it.

"What is this?"

"A watch."

"What is it made of?"

"Gold."

And so on, until Zingo had described it as a lady's wrist watch, with the monogram J. A. on the back, whose hands pointed to nine-thirty, and whose crystal was cracked.

At first Freddy couldn't figure out what kind of a code Presto was using to communicate with Zingo. For all mind-reading teams use a code of some kind or other. The one who goes through the audience may signal by the way he holds his hands, or by holding his head up or down or to one side or the other; or he may use a code in which the words he uses stand for different things, or qualities of things. Many of these codes are very long and complicated, and sometimes several codes may be combined, so that even though you know a code is being used, it is impossible to tell what it is.

Presto was clowning a good deal as he passed through the audience. He danced around a lot and his ears were in constant motion, but his questions were always about the same, so Freddy didn't think that they concealed any code. But the ears! It came to Freddy suddenly that the rabbit was really using his ears as signal flags, wigwagging information about the various objects to Zingo.

Freddy didn't interrupt Zingo's performance, but when it was over, he came forward. He could explain, he said, how this mind reading had been done. But as he had told them the week before, no reputable magician will ever publicly explain another magician's tricks. "However," he said, "I don't need to explain. In order to win the hundred dollars, I have merely to give you a better mind-reading performance. Which I shall now proceed to do."

He took a large cone made of black paper, and after turning it this way and that, to show that it was quite empty, put it on his head. "This," he said, "is my mind-reading cap." Then he sat down in a chair, with his eyes blindfolded, and Jinx and Minx went down the aisles, each in turn picking out an article for him to describe. They said nothing except: "I have an article, Professor Frederico," and then Freddy would tell them all about it, even giving the addresses and postmark dates on letters, and reading sentences that people had written on cards.

It was a pretty impressive exhibition. Since he could not see the cats, it was evident that they were not signalling to him; and as they never spoke except in the same form of words, even

Zingo could not discover that any verbal code was being used.

Now the way Freddy worked it was this: he had clipped off the tip of the paper cone so that there was a hole large enough to admit a wasp. Jacob and Eph and Fritz cruised about above the heads of the audience with their wings just idling so that they wouldn't make the angry buzz that wasps' wings make when they're really out on business. If anyone saw them, they just thought they were moths that had flown in, attracted by the light. When one of the cats picked out an article, one of the wasps would glide down and light on his shoulder, and then, having got full information, would fly back in a roundabout way and light on the tip of the cone, and shout his information down the hole. For the cap was really a megaphone, which made the sound of the wasp's voice loud enough so Freddy could hear it.

All in all, Freddy described some twenty articles; then he took off the blindfold and the cap, and said: "Now, ladies and gentlemen, to whom do you award the money?" And the audience shouted: "Freddy! Freddy wins!"

Zingo made several objections; he said there were earphones in the caps; he tried to prove in various ways that Freddy had cheated. But the audience had made up its mind, and Mr. Weezer paid the money over.

So Freddy came forward, and he thanked everybody, and he said: "My friends, I have now got back all but ten dollars of the money Signor Zingo took from me last week. But I've had a good deal more than ten dollars' worth of fun here tonight, and I will now turn the rest of the program over to Signor Zingo. I know that he has a great many more interesting tricks up his sleeve, and I hope you will stay and enjoy them." And bowing right and left as the audience rose in their seats to applaud him, he walked down the aisle and left the theatre.

Leo and Mr. Boomschmidt and Bill Wonks joined Freddy outside the theatre, and they went into Dixon's Diner and had a sandwich together. Leo took off the long shawl that he had disguised himself with so that Zingo wouldn't recognize him, and Freddy took off his war bonnet and his magician's coat, and Mr. Boomschmidt took off his plug hat, and Bill loosened his necktie, and they sat in their booth and ate and chatted comfortably. Mr. Boomschmidt was enthusiastic about Freddy's per-

*The cap was really a megaphone.*

formance. "My goodness," he said, "you're three times the magician Zing is—I don't know but four times, eh, Leo?"

"You work it out, chief," said the lion. "I was never any good at figures."

"It certainly did my heart good," Mr. Boomschmidt said, "the way you clipped his whiskers tonight. The things I've put up with from him —caused me more trouble!—and then stole all the petty cash. But I guess it was worth a thousand dollars to get rid of him."

"I felt sort of sorry for him, though," Freddy said. "Oh, I know he's a crook, but he's really a good magician, and proud of it, I suppose; and when everything went wrong in front of all those people . . ."

Leo let out a roar. "Well, file my claws!" he said. "You going soft on us, pig? Sorry because he got back what he stole off you? I guess you been writing too much poetry lately."

"Leo's right," said Mr. Boomschmidt. "Zing's a crook—a real bad man, Freddy. He deserves a lot worse than you gave him. And my goodness, you watch out for him. I'd just as soon have a tiger mad at me as Zing—sooner, I guess, considering what nice folks tigers usually are."

A shadow fell across the table and they looked

up to see Mr. Groper looming over them. "Hail and good evening," said the hotelkeeper gloomily. "I saw that prestidigitative extravaganza of yours this evening," he said to Freddy. "Very masterfully excogitated and performed. I guess your fiscal deficit is about expunged."

"Just about," said Freddy after a glance into his dictionary. "Look, Mr. Groper; I suppose you're mad at me, and I guess you have a right to be. I haven't done very much about getting rid of Signor Zingo for you. But I'm going to. Somehow or other, I'll get him out of your hotel."

"I ain't mad," said Mr. Groper. "Just, as you might say, kind of reduced to the nadir of pessimistic hypochondriasis."

"Good gracious," said Mr. Boomschmidt, "what lovely words! Leo, write those down, will you? Can't you see them on a billboard? On *your* billboard, Leo; my goodness, they're just what we need to pep up the description of you. Great Bald African Lion—that's kind of weak. Lots of people wouldn't cross the street nowadays to see a lion, no matter how bald. But the 'Great Bald African Nadir,' and underneath, 'the ferocious Pessimisticus Hypochondriasis, terror of the jungle,'—"

"The nadir's a kind of antelope, isn't he chief?" Leo said.

"The nadir," put in Mr. Groper, "is the ultimate and nethermost profundity of the abyss."

"There, what did I tell you, Leo?" said Mr. Boomschmidt.

"Intellectually speaking," Mr. Groper added.

"See?" said Mr. Boomschmidt. "You're a lot more intellectual than most lions."

"Look, chief—you leave me out of this," said Leo. "Why don't you ask Mr. Groper to sit down and have a cup of coffee?"

Mr. Groper used the complete resources of his mental dictionary to thank them and inform them that he couldn't stay; and after he had shaken hands all around to show there was no hard feeling, he left.

Freddy had been feeling pretty good, but the sight of Mr. Groper made him feel guilty. He had promised Mr. Groper his help, but tonight he had been fighting his own battle, not the hotelkeeper's. And what was worse, he couldn't think of any way of getting Zingo to leave the hotel. "I suppose," he said, "I'll have to go see Old Whibley again."

His friends agreed that that was the best thing to do, and they all got into the big red car and drove out to the Bean farm. While the others went in to have a piece of cake and another cup of coffee with the Beans, Freddy trotted up towards the woods.

He was just above the duck pond when a big silent shape drifted across in front of him, and Whibley's voice said: "Good show tonight. Congratulate you."

The owl was gone before Freddy could answer. "Whibley!" he shouted. "Please, Whibley; I want to talk to you!"

Whibley didn't reply; evidently he had gone home. But as Freddy started on he saw two small white shapes approaching through the darkness, and a subdued but excitable quacking told him that it was the two ducks, Alice and Emma, returning from the show.

They had caught sight of him. "Oh, Freddy, such a delightful evening!" said Alice. "You and that Mr. Zingo make a wonderful team!"

"Such a clever idea," said Emma; "each pretending to do better tricks than the other! Are you going into partnership with him? I do think you'd make your fortunes!"

"Hey, wait a minute!" Freddy said. "That wasn't pretending." And he quickly explained the situation to them.

"Dear me, we had no idea!" said Alice. "What an unpleasant character he is, to be sure!" And Emma said: "How silly we were, sister! Of course—he's the horrid man that broke into our bank!"

Old Whibley's voice floated down to them from a tree that overhung the pond. "You want to see me, pig, or are you going to stand there talking all night? If so, I'm going home."

"Oh, I called you and you didn't answer, and I thought you'd gone," said Freddy.

"Would have gone," said the owl. "Only I knew you'd probably come and kick my door down. What do you want to know this time— how much two times two is? That's about as important as your questions usually are."

"I want to know how to get Zingo to leave the hotel," Freddy said. "He's ruining Mr. Groper's business. Whenever Mr. Groper asks him to pay his bill, he pretends to find a caterpillar or a beetle on his plate, and threatens to tell everybody about it. Of course if it got around that the hotel was careless about the food, nobody would eat there any more. So Mr. Groper is scared, and lets Zingo live there free."

"Why doesn't Mr. Groper really put caterpillars on Mr. Zingo's plate?" Emma asked. "Then *he* wouldn't want to eat there any more."

"Upon my word!" Old Whibley exclaimed. "Out of the mouths of babes and ducklings! You've got the root of the matter, Emma. But why," he asked curiously, "do you think that would work?"

"Why, dear me, it stands to reason doesn't it?" said the duck. "If Mr. Zingo wanted to make people stop eating there, he would say to himself: 'What would make *me* stop eating there?' "

Whibley said emphatically: "Right! There's your answer, pig."

"Is it?" said Freddy. "I don't see it. Zingo'd know it was just the same trick he'd played on Groper. He's just laugh."

"He might laugh but he wouldn't eat anything," Alice said.

Whibley clattered his beak irritably. "Preserve me from dumb pigs!" he said. "Zingo wants to make folks shudder. So he picks out caterpillars. Why? Because they make *him* shudder. Q.E.D., and goodnight," he said, and flew off.

"I'm afraid we must go in, Freddy," said Emma. "This night air—dear me, I just *can't* get used to this modern idea that night air is harmless. Why look at Uncle Wesley! He *never* opens his window at night, even in summer, and you know how robust *he* is! Goodnight, Freddy, and thanks for a lovely evening."

Freddy trotted back to the barnyard.

## Chapter 19

At three the next afternoon, when the hotel diningroom was empty, Mr. Groper unlocked the door and admitted Freddy and Jinx. They carried a little wooden box and a hammer and nails, and they went to work on the table that was reserved for Zingo.

Mr. Groper sat and watched them gloomily. "Pity I ain't been indoctrinated with imperishable optimism," he said. "This here enterprise involves an unjustifiably prodigal expense, both temporal and operose."

"Ain't it the truth?" said Jinx. "Through, Freddy? Well, come on."

That evening at dinnertime, when Zingo came into the dining room, he gave a start, stopped short for a minute, then went on to his table. For seated at Mr. Groper's table were Freddy—in war bonnet and Indian suit again— and the sheriff. The butt of a pistol stuck out of the sheriff's pocket. Of course it was just a butt, which was sewn into the pocket without any pistol attached to it. But Zingo didn't know that.

Freddy had asked the sheriff to have dinner with him in order to have protection in case Zingo attacked him. He had worn the Indian clothes so as not to disturb the hotel guests, some of whom, being from out of town, might be startled to see a pig dining at the next table. But he didn't try to hide now, and he sat facing the magician.

Zingo must have known that something was afoot, but he gave no sign. He ordered, and when his soup was brought, dipped his spoon in the plate—and then shoved his chair back with an "Arrrrrh!" of distaste. Then he beckoned to Mr. Groper.

The hotelkeeper, followed by Freddy and the sheriff, went over to his table.

"Look here, Groper," he exclaimed; "what do you call this?" And he pointed to a fuzzy brown caterpillar which was crawling towards the edge of the table.

The three peered at it.

"Inexistent and non-dimensional," said Mr. Groper.

"There's nothing there," said Freddy.

"What do *you* call it, mister?" asked the sheriff.

"What do *I* call it!" shouted the magician. "A great nasty caterpillar, that's what I call it, Groper! And I demand . . . !"

"Shut up!" the sheriff snapped. As the caterpillar crawled off over the edge of the table he turned to the other diners. "Gentlemen," he said, "Signor Zingo has been claiming for a long time that he has found caterpillars and other varmints on the plates of food that are brought in to him from the kitchen. He's made these claims and tried to give the hotel a bad name. Now he's tried it again. I call you gentlemen to witness—there's nothing here. Will some of you step over here and look?"

Two or three men got up and came over. They looked on top and under the table, and on the floor where Zingo claimed the caterpillar must have dropped, but found nothing.

"But I *saw* it!" Zingo insisted. "It was right there!"

"When folks see things that ain't there," said one of the men significantly, "they get taken off to the hospital in a little wagon."

"Guess he's got caterpillars inside his head," said another, and they went back to their tables.

But five minutes later the same thing happened. This time it was a beetle. And the third time it was another beetle, and the other diners began to get annoyed.

"Look here, Mister," said one, "if you want to watch bugs, go outdoors and let us eat in peace."

The fourth time it was another caterpillar, and Zingo left the room without finishing his meal.

Now of course this was what Freddy had done: he had fastened the little wooden box to the under side of Zingo's table, in the corner by one leg where nobody would notice it even if they got underneath. Inside the box were the caterpillars and beetles whom the mice had found in Zingo's room, and who had offered Freddy their help. Volunteered for foreign service, as Jinx said. Freddy had given them their instructions, and as soon as Zingo was seated at the table one would crawl out, across the table, then down into the box again. Every five minutes this was to go on as long as Zingo was in the dining room.

It was a dangerous service they had volunteered for. But Freddy had posted Jacob in the dining room with instructions to divert Zingo's attention if he attacked or attempted to sqush one of the volunteers. Fortunately the magician was too horrified and disgusted by the bugs to want to sqush them.

At breakfast and at lunch the next day the performance was repeated. By this time Zingo was hungry. He went over to Dixon's Diner, but Mr. Dixon had heard about how he was abusing Mr. Groper's hospitality and made him pay in advance for everything he ate. When he had finished, Mr. Dixon said: "Don't come in here again, mister." Mr. Dixon had a butcher knife in his hand so Zingo didn't ask him what he meant.

Dinner on the second day finished the magician. He came in and sat down at his table, but although no caterpillars or beetles appeared, he shuddered so in anticipation of their appearance that he couldn't hold his soup spoon, and in a few minutes he left and went up to his room. The mice, who were still posted in Freddy's old room, reported that he was packing.

"That's all right," said Freddy. "I heard this morning that he tried to get a room at Mrs. Peppercorn's. But she wouldn't take him. I don't believe anybody else would, either; he'll have to leave town. That's all right too, but he still owes Mr. Groper ninety dollars. Check up if you can, Eeny, and see if he has that much left."

"Yeah, he has," said Eeny. "You remember that hundred he had hidden in his suitcase? I saw him count it and put it in his pocket."

"Oh dear," said Freddy, "he'll probably leave town today, then. If we could only get him alone —but I don't see how we can, and anyway there aren't enough of us to handle him."

"Leo would help us," said Jinx. "He hasn't gone back to Binghamton yet; they're having such a good time at the jail that Mr. Boomschmidt decided to stay a couple days longer."

"I hate to let him get away without paying," Freddy said; "but even with Leo I don't see what we could do."

They were in Mr. Groper's private office at the hotel—the cats, two of the mice, the spiders, the bug volunteers, and Freddy. They all looked pretty gloomy, even the caterpillars, although they haven't much in the way of faces to look gloomy with, and aren't really very emotional anyway. And Cousin Augustus darted in.

"He's leaving tonight on the eight-fifteen bus," the mouse panted. "Just heard him tell Presto."

"Well, I guess we're sunk," said Jinx.

"Wait a minute!" said Freddy. "That bus station is by the drugstore, up Main Street; opposite it there's a vacant lot, isn't there? Come on, Jinx, let's walk up and look at the place; I've got an idea."

Carrying his two suitcases and the bag in which Presto traveled, Signor Zingo left the hotel at quarter to eight to walk up Main Street to the bus station. He didn't know it was quarter to eight; he thought it was eight o'clock, because at Freddy's request, Mr. Groper had set the hotel clock ahead quarter of an hour. He was angry when he got to the station and found how early it was. He put his bags down outside the drugstore and sat on them, then he lit one of his long thin cigars and sat looking out across the vacant lot on the opposite side of the street.

Suddenly something caught his eye. Behind

the stone wall on the far side of the lot something moved. He watched, idly at first, then with more interest as a head wearing an Indian war bonnet came up above the wall. Then a figure —which he couldn't see very clearly because it was beginning to grow dark—climbed the wall and came dancing towards him. It wore an Indian suit, and it flapped its arms and made insulting gestures. "Yaaaah!" it shouted. "The big brave magician! Chased out of town by a big bad caterpillar! Haw, haw, haw! Who got kissed by a wasp!"

One or two people who had been standing around in front of the drugstore laughed, and one of them said: "Look out, mister; he'll hypnotize you again."

"Maybe he'll make you pay your hotel bill," said the sheriff, who was leaning against the side of the building, chewing a straw.

Zingo sneered at him. "If he can make me pay anything after the way I have been treated, I'll eat my hat."

The figure in the Indian suit thumbed his nose at the magician, and sang:

*Zingo, Stingo had a new trick:*
*Kissed the wasps and made them sick.*

*When the wasps came out to sting*
*Zingo ran like anything!*

And he sang:

*Zing was in his bedroom, counting stolen*
*money;*
*Zing was in his bedroom, talking to his bunny;*
*Zing came out upon the stage, in his best clothes,*
*And along came a big wasp and stung him on*
*the nose!*

And he sang:

*Sing a song of Zingo, pocket full of lies;*
*Four and twenty waspses, baked in a pie.*
*When the pie was opened the wasps began to*
*sting.*
*Wasn't that a pretty dish to set before old Zing?*

Zingo snarled at the crowd, which had grown larger, and was laughing heartily. He half-turned to pick up his bags and go inside the store. Then suddenly his temper blew up—as Freddy had been sure it would. He whirled and started running across the street towards his tormentor. The sheriff said: "Here, none of that, now!" and ran after him.

The Indian suit turned and ran too; it flopped across the wall and ducked down just as Zingo caught up. The magician vaulted the wall—and felt himself seized and held motionless by two immensely powerful forepaws. And a deep voice said: "Well, dye my hair if it isn't old Zing! Hello, Zing; how's the sorcery business?"

Of course it was not Freddy at all, as, in the dim light, Zingo had supposed, but Leo, wearing Freddy's war bonnet and Indian suit—which aside from being rather short in the sleeves, wasn't much too tight for him. Freddy was a rather portly pig.

"Dear old Zing!" said Leo, and hugged him. "My, it's good to see you again!" And he gave him another hug.

Zingo's breath went out of him with a Whoosh! He couldn't have spoken even if he had had anything to say. The sheriff, who had come up, sat down on the wall and looked on with a pleased expression.

"Well, well; nothing to say to your old pal?" said the lion. "Kind of overcome with happiness, I expect. Well, let's just sit down here a while and talk about old times."

"Let me go!" Zingo panted. "I—I'll miss my bus. Sheriff, I appeal to you—"

*"Dear old Zing!" said Leo, and hugged him.*

"I'll make a note of it," said the sheriff indifferently.

"Lots of time," said Leo. "I've got something for you—a little going-away present, you might say. Just reach in my pocket and pull out that paper."

Zingo obeyed. The paper was a bill for ninety dollars for board and lodging, marked "Paid in full," and signed by Mr. Groper.

"Isn't that nice of Groper?" said Leo. "He knew you wouldn't feel right about going away without settling your bill. And of course we all know how absent-minded you are."

"Ninety dollars!" Zingo said. "I haven't got any ninety dollars. You tell Mr. Groper . . ."

"Oh, pooh!" said Leo. "What's ninety dollars to a magician? Just a few passes in the air and there's your ninety bucks, right in your hand."

"But I tell you," Zingo began—

And then Leo growled. It wasn't a loud growl, but it was so low, so ferocious, that Zingo shivered. "All right," he said in a dull voice. "Let go my arm." He felt in an inside pocket and brought out the money.

"Well, well," said the sheriff; "there's one other little formality, and then you can get your bus. Come along, mister."

"Hey, what's all this?" Zingo demanded. "You can't hold me here. I—" He stopped and stared as Freddy and Mr. Groper came out from behind a shed that stood a little way above the wall, and walked down to the group. "This is a conspiracy!" he said. "Sheriff, I demand your protection."

"Sure, sure," said the sheriff. "Don't you worry—I'll protect you. That's what the law's for—to give you protection. And also to see that you keep your promises. Like paying bills, and so on."

"Well, I've paid my hotel bill," said Zingo. "What more do they want?"

"There's another promise you just made," said the sheriff. "About your hat. Remember? You were going to eat it. Twice you've promised that. Now you've got to come through."

Zingo protested violently, but Leo and the sheriff took him by the arms and led him down to the drugstore. They made him unpack his hat; then they took him into the store and sat him on the end stool at the soda fountain, and they cut the hat up with scissors and put it on a plate and salted and peppered it.

"O K, now eat it up," said Leo.

Zingo looked with distaste at his plate. "I—I

can't," he said. "Anyway, you'll make me miss my bus."

"If you eat fast you'll catch it all right," said the sheriff.

The magician put a piece of the hat in his mouth and chewed and swallowed it. Then he started on a second piece. Just then the bus drove up. Zingo tried to get down from his stool, but Leo pushed him back on and held him. The bus passengers, when they heard what was going on, got out and crowded into the drugstore, and after the driver had blown his horn a few times, he shrugged his shoulders and got out and joined the crowd.

Freddy turned to Leo: "I think we ought to let him go," he said. "He's had enough."

"Well, crack my incisors!" said the lion. "Going soft on us again?" He stared at Zingo, who was doggedly chewing his third bit of hat. "We've got to teach him a lesson. Besides, it's the first time he's eaten anything he's paid for himself in a long time. Still and all," he added thoughtfully, "we don't want the guy to get sick."

"Inadvisable to produce digestive disturbances," Mr. Groper agreed.

So they let Zingo off. The passengers crowded

back, shouting and laughing, into the bus, and Freddy helped Zingo stuff the remains of the hat into a suitcase. Then he took a ten dollar bill from his pocket and held it out to the magician.

"What's this?" Zingo asked suspiciously.

"For a new hat," said Freddy. "I've no wish to take more from you than we've got coming."

Zingo took the bill, folded it slowly and put it in his pocket. The anger faded out of his face. "Well," he said awkwardly, "thanks. Nobody ever gave me a break before."

"I don't quite believe that," Freddy said. "You worked for Mr. Boomschmidt, and I know he'd give you the breaks."

"Yeah," Zingo said. "I guess you're right. I've got an awful bad temper—it's always getting me into things."

Freddy didn't say anything. Zingo was just making excuses for himself; he wasn't really sorry. If nobody ever gave him a break, it was because he never gave anybody else one. There wasn't much you could do with a person like that. But Freddy had won; there was no use rubbing it in.

"Well, so long," he said. "Good luck." And Zingo got into the bus.

As they walked back to the hotel, Mr. Groper said: "I guess I got to apologize for my underestimation of the remarkable efficiency of your strategical manoeuvers, by the instrumentality of which same retributive justice has been unerringly dealt out. I also got to acknowledge gratitude, not only for monetary indemnification, but for elimination of the cause of the decrement in my assets." Here he shook Freddy by the hand. "The comestibles prepared in the culinary precincts of my caravansary are your permanent perquisites and upon demand will be served gratis in unlimited quantity to yourself and companions whether extempore or at a predetermined time. This ain't your pecuniary emolument, for which I anticipate you will render a statement, but is in the nature of an augmentation, subsidy or bonus in recognition of exceptionally sedulous assiduity combined with judicious and perspicacious opportunism. I trust you find it adequate." And he patted Freddy on the shoulder.

"Why—why, sure," said Freddy. He wasn't certain that it was the right answer. But what would you have said?

# Freddy Books Published By
# The Overlook Press

## FREDDY THE DETECTIVE
by Walter R. Brooks
ISBN 978-1-59020-418-4 • $9.99 • PB

Freddy is inspired while reading *The Adventures of Sherlock Holmes* to become a detective. Setting out with his intrepid partner Mrs. Wiggins the cow, he is ultimately challenged to prove that Jinx the cat was framed for murder.

## FREDDY THE POLITICIAN
by Walter R. Brooks
ISBN 978-1-59020-419-1 • $9.99 • PB

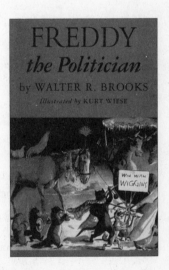

eddy, the good-natured pig with a
etic soul, is promoting a campaign
get Mrs. Wiggins, the cow, elected
esident of the First Animal Republic.
s he himself is an officer in the newly
ganized First Animal Bank, he has
ore than a modicum of influence—
he can just figure out how to use it.

THE OVERLOOK PRESS
New York, NY
www.overlookpress.com

# Freddy Books Published By
## The Overlook Press

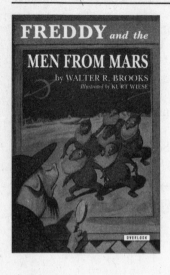

### FREDDY AND THE MEN FROM MARS
by Walter R. Brooks
ISBN 978-1-59020-695-9 • $10.99 • PB

The trouble all starts with the report in the newspaper that six little creatures, believed to be Martians, have been singlehanded captured by Herbert Garble. Freddy ever ready to maintain his reputation a detective, immediately suspects a hoax and forthwith sets out to expose it. How does so makes for one of the most hilario of all Freddy tales.

### FREDDY AND THE BASEBALL TEAM FROM MARS
by Walter R. Brooks
ISBN 978-1-59020-696-6 • $10.99 • PB

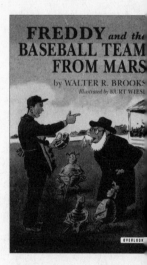

Mr. Boorschmidt's circus in Centerboro boasted a new attractiton—six real Martians. Freddy decided to help—by organizing a Martian baseball team. Anyone who can imagine a baseball team consisting of Martians, an elephant, and ostrich, with Freddy as coach, has a slight idea of what's in store.

THE OVERLOOK PRESS
New York, NY
www.overlookpress.com